What people are saying about THE ROSE TATTOO:

UNSPOKEN CONFESSIONS
"The hunt is thrilling, the passion hot, the danger only too real."
—*Affaire de Coeur*

UNLAWFULLY WEDDED
"Extremely well-done."
—*Rendezvous*

UNDYING LAUGHTER
"Kelsey Roberts displays a glorious sense of humor in UNDYING LAUGHTER...."
—Debbie Richardson, *Romantic Times*

HANDSOME AS SIN
"Kelsey Roberts once again delivers sparkling dialogue and great touches of humor."
—Debbie Richardson, *Romantic Times*

THE TALL, DARK ALIBI
"The plot is exciting, the hero dangerous, and the chemistry! It was so good I hated to reach the last page."
—Laurel Gainer, *Affaire de Coeur*

THE SILENT GROOM
"Kelsey Roberts will take you on a fun, fanciful and fascinating journey.... If you are looking for romance and intrigue with a twist, you won't want to miss her."
—Nora Roberts

THE WRONG MAN
"Roberts employs a masterful talent for hooking the reader with incredible suspense..."
—*Gothic Journal*

HER MOTHER'S ARMS
"Talented Kelsey Roberts masterfully blends the old and the new in HER MOTHER'S ARMS."
—Debbie Richardson, *Romantic Times*

Dear Reader,

I can't believe the Rose Tattoo has been open for three years now. I introduced this series with Shelby and Dylan and I'm proud to announce the birth of their third child in *Unforgettable Night*. So the baby wouldn't be the only new arrival in town, I've welcomed Dylan's brother Matthew to Charleston.

Unforgettable Night is the kind of story that I loved so dearly as a reader. Now I've been given the opportunity to tell the tale of a secret past all my own. If you're familiar with some of the other books in this series, you'll know I often get the seeds for my fantasies in fact. Well, this is no exception. I had an uncle who was injured during World War II. The injury resulted in his losing a large chunk of his memory. So I took that seed as the basis for this book. DeLancey Jones, the Rose Tattoo's chef you may have met in *Her Mother's Arms*, has a problem. She doesn't remember the first fifteen years of her life. The memory loss isn't what bothers her—it's the fear that there's a very real, very deadly reason that she can't remember a thing.

Matt Tanner is a great foil for DeLancey. Obviously a woman can't overcome the things DeLancey has without great personal strength. Needless to say, the kindling is stacked and the sparks are ready to fly when this strong-willed woman meets her match.

As always, I hope you'll enjoy this visit to the Rose Tattoo. Please let me know, by writing to Harlequin Books at 300 East 42nd Street, New York, New York 10017. Or, if you're in cyberspace, you can contact me through Harlequin's web site at http://www.romance.net. Just select author pages and you'll find me there.

Happy reading!

Kelsey Roberts

Kelsey Roberts

Unforgettable Night

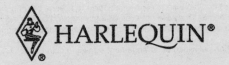

HARLEQUIN®

TORONTO • NEW YORK • LONDON
AMSTERDAM • PARIS • SYDNEY • HAMBURG
STOCKHOLM • ATHENS • TOKYO • MILAN • MADRID
PRAGUE • WARSAW • BUDAPEST • AUCKLAND

For Karen Harrison, who has helped me through some really rough times, treated my son like her own, given my husband Easter dinner while I vacationed in Kiawah, but mostly because you were a good enough friend to turn forty before me. Love you.

ISBN 0-373-22477-X

UNFORGETTABLE NIGHT

Drawing by Linda Harding Shaw

CAST OF CHARACTERS

DeLancey Jones—Her forgotten past was somehow connected to her uncertain future. Was murder the missing link?

Matthew Tanner—He'd come to solve an old crime. Would his feelings for DeLancey make him part of it?

Mrs. Esther Pembleton—She'd taken DeLancey in and given her everything, except the truth. Now she was dead.

Gomez—He'd found DeLancey that fateful night, and treated her like a daughter. He, too, died mysteriously….

Alan Faircloth—Mrs. Pembleton's attorney's primary agenda was to put DeLancey behind bars.

Steven Thomason—Alan Faircloth's associate had earned Mrs. Pembleton's trust. What had he done with it?

Dr. Charles Howard—A family friend and compassionate doctor. Or a liar and murderer…

Prologue

She opened her eyes and the first thing she noticed was the blood. The front of her dress was covered with a dark, wet stain. Instinctively, she felt her chest and stomach for wounds. That's when she found the knife.

A misting rain began as she reached into her pocket and carefully pulled the knife out by the handle. There was more blood. Panicking, she tossed the knife on the ground, then wiped her hand on the hard stone behind her.

The mist was quickly turning to rain as she stood up. Shielding her eyes with her hand, she looked around. She was alone in the cemetery, and that was almost as terrifying as the blood.

When the dark clouds opened, she raced for the nearest shelter, which happened to be a mausoleum. The beating rain had faded the stain, though her anxiety was stronger than ever.

Moving to where the rain fell from the roof in a waterfall, she held out her clothing and rinsed it clean, then did the same with her hands. She was soaked and cold, so she huddled in the structure, eyes wide as she read the names and dates on the vaults.

They were unfamiliar. In fact, everything was unfamiliar. Where was she? What had she done? She seemed to know almost nothing about herself—nothing before this moment. Then it struck her. She knew her age. She knew she was fifteen. She didn't know how, she just knew it when she read the date on one of the plaques.

She also knew she was scared. Especially when she saw a figure coming toward her. A hooded slicker covered his face, and all she could think to do was be as quiet as possible.

"I thought I saw someone down here when I was driving by," he said, smiling at her as he pushed the hood off his head and shook off some of the rain. Water pooled at his feet, and she had a flash of memory, of seeing another pool of liquid…only it wasn't rain.

She cowered against the wall, terrified even though the elderly man was looking at her with kind eyes.

"Are you lost, honey? Where are your parents?"

She blinked, understanding the question but unable to answer. It wasn't that she didn't want to answer. She just couldn't.

"Cat got your tongue?" he asked with a smile.

"No, sir."

He lifted the poncho over his head and held it out to her, saying, "Let's get you out of this weather. Mrs. Pembleton's is just a few miles down the road.

We'll get you dry and warm until your folks come for you.''

He held the slicker like a tarp and waited. "You can't stay in here, honey. You don't need to be afraid," he said as he took a step closer. "We'll call your folks and get you home lickety-split. I'm Joe Gomez, but most folks just call me plain ol' Gomez. What's your name?''

The blood. The knife. She must have done something terrible! "DeLancey," she said, reading from one of the memorial plaques. "DeLancey Jones.''

She offered a weak smile as she moved toward him. He chuckled. "For a minute there I thought you'd forgotten your own name.''

She couldn't look him in the eyes because the truth was, she had.

Chapter One

Ten years later

"C'mon, DeLancey," Matt pleaded, following her around the kitchen. "You've already turned me down twenty-six times in less than a month."

"Twenty-seven," she corrected without looking up from the cooler she was filling.

Either she was satisfied with her efforts, or the cooler could hold no more of the frozen leftovers from the Rose Tattoo's kitchen. Matt didn't really care, since the result was she could no longer avoid looking at him. When she finally lifted her face to his, he felt what he'd come to call "the jolt." It was the same each time. In all his thirty-three years, he had never felt such an overpowering attraction to a woman. Unfortunately for him, *this* woman showed no signs of succumbing to the charm he'd been lavishing on her.

She gave him her kiss-off smile, but Matt completely missed the message, distracted by the sexy mole just above and to the left of her upper lip. The small imperfection seemed to add an exotic touch to her otherwise flawless beauty.

She placed her hands on her hips, then tilted her head to one side. The action caused dark mahogany hair to spill over her bare shoulder. "I'll bet striking out twenty-seven consecutive times is a first for you, Professor."

"It is," he admitted as he tried to keep the tattered remnants of his ego intact. "But anything worth having is worth working for."

Her smile faded. "What part of 'I'm not interested' don't you understand?" She punctuated the remark by using her foot to close the lid of the cooler.

Matt studied her expression, knowing on a purely gut level that she was lying. Well, maybe not lying, but he hadn't forgotten a single thing that had passed between them since their first meeting. And he sure as hell hadn't forgotten the fleeting spark of attraction he had initially seen in her eyes. He just couldn't figure out why she had gone from hot to cold for no apparent reason.

"Okay," he said on a breath of frustration. "What's the harm in me tagging along with you?"

"Mrs. Pembleton is ill," she answered. "I don't think she will appreciate my bringing a houseguest without notice."

Matt grinned. "So call her. I'm assuming the tiny southern hamlet of Canfield has phones, right?"

She gave him a reproachful glare. "It may not be New York, Professor, but contrary to your ignorant misconceptions, Canfield isn't a town full of good ol' boys in trailers.'' Her sensuous Southern accent became artificially exaggerated as she continued. ''We even have a few houses that don't have old rusted refrigerators in the front yard, and we stopped marrying our cousins a couple years back.''

Pensively, he stroked his chin while fighting a grin. ''That's why I want to spend time with you. I have so much to learn.''

Her wicked smile returned. ''Why don't you start by learning to take no for an answer?''

''You know how pushy we New Yorkers can be. Come on, DeLancey. I need someone to show me the area. I'd rather not waste time trying to navigate quaint, poorly marked back roads when you're going up there anyway. Please? It's not like I'm asking you to jump into bed with me.'' He felt a tad smug when a faint reddish blush colored her cheeks. ''Though of course, I'm game if you are.''

DeLancey rolled her eyes. ''And you wonder why I'm not interested in playing tour guide.''

She turned and began cleaning off the shiny stainless-steel work station. Matt let out a slow breath as he watched her. In the heat of the July sun, DeLancey Jones wasn't wearing her white chef's hat or her white, double-breasted uniform. It was the first time in their month's acquaintance she hadn't been decked out in both—and it was like he was seeing her for the first time. Especially when his eyes drifted to where the hem of her soft denim shorts met long, well-toned thighs. The woman had incredible legs.

''Stop leering, Professor,'' she said.

He couldn't tell if it was humor or sarcasm he'd heard in her tone. "I was admiring, not leering."

DeLancey glanced over her shoulder at him. Her pretty face was fresh and innocent, yet there was a flicker of what his mother called "the devil" in those big brown eyes. A fringe of dark hair feathered her face, a stunning complement to her olive complexion. He was sure the style was meant to be practical, but the mussed, tousled strands gave her a just-got-out-of-bed look that had inspired more than a few fantasies during his first month in Charleston.

Her lashes fluttered above the rims of the small, round glasses that slipped to the tip of her nose almost immediately after she'd put them on. She had beautiful eyes, yet as he stood staring at her, Matt thought he recognized the faint traces of pain shrouded in the layers of cocky self-assurance. It wasn't the first time he had noted that hint of hidden unhappiness in her expression. But his intuition also told him DeLancey wasn't the bare-your-soul type.

"You were right," he said, ramming his hands into the front pockets of his slacks. It was a defensive move—he was afraid of his irresistible urge to touch her.

"About what?" she asked. Lowering her eyes, DeLancey went to work whisking some sort of chocolate mixture.

"I've never been turned down twenty-seven times."

"This morning makes twenty-eight," she corrected briskly, though he could recognize a glint of humor in her voice.

"Whatever. You're killing my ego here, De-Lancey." He moved to stand across from her as she scraped the sweet mixture into a baking pan. "How about a compromise?"

"What kind of compromise?" she asked before she placed the pan into the oven.

"Take me with you, and I promise to behave."

When she turned to face him, she brushed hair off her forehead and pushed her glasses into place. The yellow-tinted lenses hid her eyes. "I don't think you know how to behave."

"Cut me a break here. All I want is an opportunity to talk to you—purely in the name of gaining a local perspective for my research—and it doesn't make sense for both of us to drive all that way alone."

"I like to be alone," she countered.

Her head tilted as she leaned against the stainless-steel oven door. Matt stepped forward and reached out with the perfectly respectable intention of wiping the smudge of cocoa powder from her cheek. The instant he felt her warm, supple skin under the pad of his thumb, respectable went right out the door. His fingers rested beneath her uplifted chin and he watched, fascinated, as her lips parted.

"No touching," she said. There was a slight hoarseness to her voice.

He wondered what her eyes looked like behind the shield of those damned glasses.

"It's against the law for an employer to touch an employee."

Reluctantly, Matt let his hand drop to his side.

"I'm not your employer and I was just getting a smudge off your face."

She shrugged her slender shoulders, then stepped to the sink. "You were coming on to me—*again.*"

Matt raked his fingers through his hair. "I prefer to think of it as an act of kindness."

When she turned, her expression gave him a surge of hope. The corners of her rosy lips twitched as she apparently battled the urge to smile. "Copping a feel is an act of kindness? I think you need a little sensitivity training. It isn't politically correct these days for a man to touch a woman without her express invitation."

He grinned at her. "Since when is sensitivity training a prerequisite for harmless dating rituals?"

DeLancey crossed her arms and continued to stare at him. At least he *thought* she was looking at him. He would have enjoyed taking those tinted glasses and grinding them into little bits beneath his heel. He hated not being able to read her expression.

"We aren't dating," she answered. "Not now, not ever. I have a strict policy against mixing business with pleasure."

His chest puffed out proudly as he taunted, "So you admit that going out with me would be a pleasure?"

Her first response was to purse her lips in a sexy pout that managed to raise his blood pressure yet again. Maybe he really did have a problem. It wasn't like him to pressure a woman, especially one who enjoyed shredding his ego at every turn.

"Figure of speech," she said. "I don't know if

going out with you would be a pleasure or not. I just know that I'm not interested in finding out.''

"So you've said," he conceded. "If you take me to Canfield with you, I promise I won't ask you out ever again. It's a win-win situation," he reasoned. "We'll be on the road, then at Mrs. Pembleton's, then I'll head off to Camden. It isn't even like you'll be alone with me for long.''

"That still doesn't get us past the fact that I'm an employee here at the Rose Tattoo.''

Matt let out a frustrated oath. "I'm not your employer.''

"You're guilty by association," she insisted. "Shelby is your sister-in-law.''

"Shelby isn't even actively working right now. She won't care. In fact, she asks me every day what kind of progress I'm making with you.''

She pulled her glasses off and gaped at him. "You actually told Shelby that I've been brushing you off?''

He nodded. "Of course. And Dylan has been ragging me for weeks. If you do this for me, I get Shelby and Dylan off my back and you get my solemn word that I'll leave you alone from here on out.''

"Swear?''

Matt could have leaped with joy. Instead, he settled for crossing his heart as he said, "Scout's honor.''

She looked at him with apprehension. "Were you ever a scout?''

He nodded. "Every young man in Loganville was required to be a scout.''

She disappeared inside the large walk-in refrigerator, reappearing a minute later balancing a stack of assorted vegetables. DeLancey was impressive with a knife. She chopped and julienned the ingredients faster and more uniformly than most people could manage with a pricey food processor. "Is Loganville a small town?"

Matt hoisted himself onto the counter that lined the far wall. He knew that when the restaurant was open, the space was used for setting up and decorating plates of DeLancey's creations before their delivery into the adjoining dining room. On this morning, it was a perch from which he had an unobstructed view of all her assets, specifically the nonculinary ones. The thin, sleeveless cotton shirt wasn't the least bit formfitting, yet there were times when she moved that the fabric hugged the outline of the most incredible body he had ever seen. He couldn't find a single flaw. And he had looked long and hard trying.

"Midsize. How about you? Were you born in Canfield?"

Her expert rhythm with the knife faltered, and she let out a small curse as she lifted her finger to her mouth.

Matt moved to her side, took her hand and examined the wound. "It's pretty deep," he said.

DeLancey pulled her hand away with a jerk and went to the sink. "It's just a nick," she said, flipping on the faucet. "A little antiseptic and a bandage and I'll be fine."

"Where's the first-aid kit?"

"On the wall in the pantry," she said.

"Keep pressure on it," he instructed. "I think it needs a stitch or two."

"I thought you were working on a doctorate in criminal justice. I didn't know it included a crash course in medicine."

"Are you always so snippy?" he asked after he had retrieved the kit.

The small tremble he felt as he took her hand in his was moderately satisfying. At least he hoped it was a sign that she wasn't as immune to him as she would have him believe. It was just the sort of salve his bruised ego needed.

"I still think this needs a stitch."

"No, it doesn't," she insisted. "Ouch!"

"Sorry," he murmured, trying to focus on patting the bleeding wound dry. His task was complicated by her scent. It was subtle, floral...and a surprise. De-Lancey apparently didn't bother with makeup, so he hadn't expected perfume. Then again, he hadn't expected his body's quick and intense reaction to merely tending her injury.

Matt made a butterfly bandage from the medical tape and wrapped her finger in a protective shell of soft gauze.

"Enough already, Professor," she said as she broke the contact. "At this rate, I'll end up looking like the mummy."

"Just trying to do a diligent job."

"Thank you."

"And please stop calling me professor. Every time you do it, I feel like looking behind me for Gilligan or the Skipper."

She offered an impish grin. "I would have thought you'd be more interested in Ginger or Mary Ann."

"Cute."

"Thanks," she purred, before going back to hiding behind her tinted lenses.

She slipped away, and Matt was again surprised by the intensity of his desire to be near her, to touch her. The thought of being close to DeLancey Jones was becoming something of an obsession. Even when he wasn't thinking of lame excuses to spend time in the Rose Tattoo's kitchen, she still managed to dominate his thoughts. Maybe Dylan was right. Maybe he did need professional help.

"Why are you frowning?" she asked, bringing him out of his fog.

"I was just thinking of something my brother said."

She smiled. It wasn't a huge grin, just a small, sensual movement of her lips that caused a knot in his gut. "I'm surprised Dylan and Shelby can even have adult conversations," she said. "I couldn't imagine having three children under four."

"You're an only child?"

She seemed to stiffen slightly before saying, "Yes."

"My folks had six kids in eight years."

"It took them that long to figure out what caused it?" she teased.

"Just good Catholics," he answered.

"Where are you in the birth order?"

"Right in the middle."

"That explains it," she said over the sudden buzz of the oven timer.

"Explains what?"

"Your second career."

Matt smiled. "How do you know that I'm on my second career?"

"Shelby mentioned it."

"Gee, she said you asked." The deep red stain on her cheeks when she turned to put the hot pan on a waiting wire rack was delightful to behold. "Was my proper Southern sister-in-law fibbing?"

He was fairly certain she was glaring at him. "I might have asked a question or two. Just to be polite."

"Your bottom lip twitches when you lie."

Instantly, DeLancey drew her lip between her teeth, then allowed it to slip out slowly. "Okay, so I asked about you when you first arrived. Back then I didn't know you were a persistent jerk."

"I'm wounded," he said, melodramatically clutching his chest.

"Not yet, but you will be if you try anything funny on the way to Canfield."

"So you'll allow me to go with you?"

"So long as you stick to the terms of the deal. We spend these two days together—platonically—and then you go away—permanently." She smiled broadly, and it rankled more than he cared to admit.

Matt frowned. "What if we have a good time together?"

"It won't matter. I'm not going to date the boss's brother-in-law. It isn't proper."

"Are all Southern beauties hung up on proper?" he asked.

"I'm very Southern. Which means that even if you

weren't related to my boss, I still would have no interest in being a temporary amusement while you flit around the state digging up painful memories, pretending it has some value as academia.''

"Whoa! Want to tell me why my research inspires your anger? Especially since Shelby told me you had—her words—a rather grim interest in old crimes.''

She looked at her hands, clenched around a tightly wrung towel. He noted her knuckles had gone white. ''I just don't see how society will be a better place once you publish your tome on unsolved murders in South Carolina. I also don't think you've given any thought to how all your digging might affect the relatives of the victims. Dylan said you used to be a cop. I would have thought you might have developed a little compassion for victims' families after seeing their pain firsthand.''

Matt tried to comprehend her sudden burst of temper. ''First, it isn't a tome,'' he corrected her, ''it's my doctoral dissertation. Second, I'm focusing on old cases, nothing in the last ten years. I'm going to speak personally to surviving relatives, and I'll send them copies of the manuscript when I've finished.''

''How courteous of you.''

''I have no intention of using crime scene photos or autopsy reports. My focus is on the investigative process. More to the point, on where that process broke down, enabling a killer or killers to go unpunished.''

In spite of his reasonable defense of his work, her anger seemed to increase. But why? Matt wondered.

DeLancey was a complex puzzle, which in some sick way only made her more attractive to him. He was so busy trying to figure out why a chef would have such strong feelings on victims' rights that he almost didn't catch her next tirade.

"Then you can do the talk-show circuit and make gobs of money. With your looks and your gazillion medals from the NYPD, I'm sure you'll be the darling of tabloid TV once you publish."

"My doctorate is in criminal justice," he argued, suddenly defensive. "And while I applaud your concern for victims, I hardly think you're being fair. I'm not looking to exploit anyone."

Her head dropped. She was quiet for a moment before grudgingly admitting, "So maybe I came on a little strong."

"Care to tell me why?" he asked. He had a cop's hunch that either she or the Pembleton woman she spoke of like a mother might have been a crime victim. It would explain a lot.

She shook her head. "I have nothing more to add."

He laughed softly at her apparent inability to admit there might be a thread of validity in his argument. Deciding to lighten the mood, he said, "Then we don't need to debate the merits of my work."

"Fine."

"Fine," he returned, mimicking her clipped tone. "I'll come back for you, okay?"

She nodded stoically, which he was pretty sure wasn't a good sign.

"I'll be back in an hour and a half," he said as he

moved toward her. He had intended to place a kiss on her cheek.

"I don't kiss on the first date," she said, placing her palms against his chest. Grinning at him, she added, "and I *definitely* don't kiss on the *only* date."

TALL, DARK AND DANGEROUS Matthew Tanner had been gone for a full five minutes before DeLancey was able to get her pulse back to normal. "I finally meet a man who curls my toes, and there isn't a thing I dare do about it," she grumbled as she leaned against the cool kitchen wall. "Admit it, DeLancey," she chided herself. "You wonder about him day and night. Have for weeks."

Yeah, she thought. *Mostly I wonder how he'll feel if he learns I'm a killer.*

Chapter Two

To keep her mind off Matt and all the unsettling
thoughts he inspired, DeLancey threw herself into the
task of preparing the foods Shelby had requested for
a private celebration of her new daughter's christen-
ing. The official service had taken place a month earlier in the upstate New York church where all Tanners
were christened.

The phone rang, and she grabbed it on the third
ring. "Rose Tattoo, may I help you?"

"You already have. Bless you!"

DeLancey smiled at the sound of Shelby's voice.
"For what? You haven't even seen the masterpieces
I've created for you and Dylan yet."

"Not that," Shelby insisted in an urgent whisper.
"Though I'm sure they will be incredible. I just
wanted to say thanks for taking Matt off our hands
for a few nights."

"I'm taking Matt to Canfield. Whatever he does
during his nights, he'll be doing without me."

Shelby laughed. "He'll be crushed."

"Only if he tries anything," DeLancey countered. "I told him up front that I'm providing transportation and he can stay in one of Mrs. Pembleton's guest rooms."

"How is she?" Shelby asked, her genuine concern coming through in her warm tone.

"I'm worried. She just doesn't seem well these days. But she's so stubborn. She insists she's fine. I'm hoping I can talk her into seeing a doctor."

"Good luck."

"I'll need it," DeLancey admitted. "Mrs. Pembleton doesn't like *anyone* telling her what to do."

Shelby chuckled softly. "I do hope you're successful in getting her to consult a doctor. But I was talking about Matt. He's very determined to change your opinion of him."

"Not likely."

"It's not such a bad prospect, DeLancey. He's a great guy. He also shares your macabre interest in old murder cases. Matt does have some wonderful qualities. He's honest and loyal."

"So is a dog."

"I would have thought you'd be thrilled to meet someone like him."

"You thought wrong," DeLancey said with conviction. "When is Rose coming by to get your dinner?"

"Oh, I forgot to tell you," Shelby said. "Rose is taking Chad and Cassidy, so Dylan is in charge of food."

"What are you in charge of?"

"Baby food," Shelby answered. "I'm trying to fill

Carly's bottomless pit of a stomach in hopes that she'll sleep long enough for Dylan and I to have a peaceful dinner.''

"Good luck," DeLancey said, laughing.

"You, too," Shelby countered. "Something tells me you'll need it. Tanner men can be very persuasive."

"Tanner men can be major pains in the butt."

"Nice to see you, too," Dylan Tanner announced.

DeLancey whirled to find Dylan and Matt in the open doorway. Her blush started at the roots of her hair and dripped humiliation in warm blotches down her face and neck. "Your wonderful husband and his annoying brother are here," she said into the phone as her eyes locked with Matt's gray gaze. "Enjoy your meal."

"You, too." Shelby laughed. "Sounds to me like you've got a mouthful of foot just now."

Dylan greeted her with a kind smile and a playful wink. "Has Shelby been telling tales out of school?"

DeLancey shifted her attention to Dylan as some of her embarrassment waned. "Fear not, Shelby thinks all Tanner men are perfect."

"Wise woman," Matt offered as he gave his brother a slap on the back.

"Blind woman," she grumbled. "She loves you both, Professor, which explains her inability to see your flaws."

Dylan chuckled as he lifted the foil from one of the trays. "This is incredible, DeLancey. We can't thank you enough."

She smiled at him. "It was the least I could do. I

hope you and Shelby have a terrific evening. You probably need one about now.''

Dylan's angled features revealed signs of fatigue. ''I'm just afraid that I'll reach over and start cutting Shelby's food out of habit.''

''You'll do fine. The two of you still act like newlyweds.''

''You don't know the half of it,'' Matt muttered under his breath. The comment earned him an elbow to the ribs from his older brother. ''Well!'' Matt defended himself. ''The walls aren't made of stone.''

Dylan lifted the trays. ''So go mooch off someone else,'' he suggested without any real malice.

Matt gave her a lecherous grin. ''I'm hoping that once she gets to know me better, DeLancey will take pity on me and offer asylum.''

''Absolutely. An insane asylum,'' she said sweetly. ''Make yourself useful, Professor. Grab the cooler.''

Dylan laughed. ''I think she's got your number, Matt. The only thing you're good for is manual labor.''

''Wrong. Unlike you, old man, I was blessed with brawn *and* brains,'' Matt said, lifting the heavy cooler as if it was nothing. ''And soon that will be Dr. Little Brother to you.''

Hot, humid air slapped DeLancey in the face as she followed the two Tanner men into the alley between the Rose Tattoo and the adjacent dependency, which had been converted into a nightclub. The parking lot was filled with construction materials for the planned expansion of the restaurant. Shelby and Rose had done so well in four years that they decided to buy the property next door to double the current space.

Dylan carried the trays to his Explorer, hurriedly loaded the car, then sped off, trailing a cloud of dust.

She followed Matt, watching the sway and swagger as he carted the heavy cooler toward the convertible parked next to her very practical sedan. She wondered again if taking Matt to Canfield was a good idea. Though she had felt a strong and instant attraction to the tall, dark-haired man, she knew full well the danger of striking up a friendship with him. That he had made no secret of the fact that he was open to more than friendship didn't help.

As she watched him deposit the cooler in the small space behind the bucket seats, she again considered quitting her job and going back to the safe haven of Mrs. Pembleton's estate. *But what if Matt can help me? Then I'd know who I killed.*

Matt's much-touted investigative skills could uncover the void of her first fifteen years. *Right,* DeLancey thought with disgust. *I'd know the truth, and that would be such a comfort…while I'm sitting on death row.*

Shoving all thoughts of her past to the back of her mind, she turned her attention to the here and now. It had been this coping skill that had always gotten her past the nightmare memory of being in that graveyard, covered in blood. She needed to think about Mrs. Pembleton. Thanks to the Rose Tattoo's decision to expand, she had more time to spend with the woman who had taken her into her home and nurtured her without ever once asking any questions. Her guardian's progressive weakness worried DeLancey. Maybe the extra time would be enough to talk her into seeking medical care.

"Is there a reason you're carting a bunch of leftovers with you?" Matt asked.

"Mrs. Pembleton is too old and too ill to cook for herself. Gomez comes up to the house three times a day and makes sure she eats properly. I want to make sure there's plenty of good stuff to choose from. It would probably be better if you put the food in my trunk. I promise I'll go slowly."

"We aren't taking your car." He slipped mirrored sunglasses on his slightly crooked nose.

"How am I supposed to get back?"

"I'm bringing you back. It's the gentlemanly thing to do."

Out of nervousness, DeLancey clicked the button on her keychain, and her car alarm chirped. "I don't know how long I'm staying!" she protested.

Matt smiled at her. It was weird talking to her reflection. Almost as weird as the fact that they were awkwardly standing on opposite sides of the car.

"That works out then, 'cause I don't know how long I'll be there, either. Incidentally, don't they have meals-on-wheels in Canfield?"

She gave him a reproving look. "Mrs. Pembleton wouldn't allow a stranger into her home." *Except for me.* "She's a widow, and Tillman Plantation is her private sanctuary. Besides, Rose and Shelby gave me their blessings when I asked if I could take food to her. *They* have heart," she grumbled as she opened the door and slipped into the car, only to have the backs of her thighs scorched by the hot leather. "Geez, Professor! I'll probably blister. Maybe you need to take a course on heat conductivity. Lesson one—leather seats get hot when exposed to the Carolina summer sun."

Matt slid in beside her, filling the small compartment with his broad shoulders, long legs and annoyingly masculine presence. *Why is my heart racing? Lordy!* It wasn't as if she hadn't seen a good-looking man before. The joint owners of the Rose Tattoo had more than their fair share of attractive relatives. *But they are all safely married,* she reminded herself. *And they aren't devoted to finding unpunished killers. And I don't have an overpowering urge to go to bed with any of them.*

"Ready?"

"Too ready," DeLancey admitted under her breath, ruefully. She nodded, not sure what might come out of her impulsive mouth if she dared to say more. She clicked the button on her keychain again, setting the alarm on her about-to-be-abandoned car.

She heard the rustle of fabric as he reached for the ignition. The action caused the deep blue cotton of his shirt to pull taut against his upper body. There was an outline of corded muscle that rippled all the way down to the waistband of his jeans.

Overwhelmed by a wave of desire, she decided to cover by going on the offensive. "Does the fancy college you work for pay for you to rent this thing?" she asked.

"I'm covering expenses. I'm on sabbatical, so they're paying my salary."

"Waste of good money," she murmured. "I didn't know a convertible was a necessary research tool."

The scent of his cologne teased her senses as she maneuvered herself as far away from the taunt of his closeness as was possible in the small confines of the car. She told herself the sudden rush of heat coursing through her was the result of the warm sun and not some sort of chemical reaction to this man.

"I'm doing a great deal of driving," he answered easily. "I thought I'd splurge." Shifting his considerable bulk in the seat, he studied her for a second before asking, "Is my choice of transportation another strike against me?"

DeLancey let out a breath and shook her head. "Of course not. I was just making an observation."

As she turned to pretend great interest in the trash lining the alley, Matt grasped her hand. "You were making an accusation," he replied. "Your beautiful brown eyes are capable of conveying an entire vocabulary of disdain. What's the deal? What is it about me that makes you so angry?"

"I'm not angry," DeLancey insisted, tugging her hand free.

"Are, too." He volleyed with a boyish grin. "Admit it, ma'am. You don't like me."

Rolling her eyes, DeLancey raked her fingers through her hair. "How astute, Professor. Still want to go to Canfield with me?"

He leaned toward her, blocking the morning sun with his broad shoulders. "I'd rather know why you dislike me."

"You're pushy."

"Persistent," he corrected.

"You're arrogant."

"Self-confident."

"You're a Yankee."

He laughed. "Guilty. So the root cause of your less than positive opinion of me is a war that ended more than a century ago?"

He was making her sound like an idiot. "No. I just don't like you. Call it—intuition."

His smile broadened. "I think the more correct term would be smoke screen."

"Meaning?"

Matt held his hand out to her like a gauntlet. "Come here."

DeLancey didn't move an inch. "Why?"

His wide grin produced such incredible dimples that she was glad she was sitting down. When he tugged his glasses off and looked at her with those eyes the color of a tumultuous thundercloud, she thought her bones would melt on the spot.

"You said you didn't like me, and I think I'm entitled to prove you wrong."

"How?"

"Scientific theory," he answered softly. Matt moved closer on a breeze of musky cologne and masculinity that could have been classified as lethal weapons. Slowly, with a sensuality that was probably as natural to him as breathing, he took several strands of her hair between his thumb and forefinger. "I have developed a hypothesis," he whispered when his face was close to hers. "Wanna hear it?"

Barely able to choke out the word no, DeLancey

wished there was some way to alleviate the sexual tension that suddenly seemed to engulf them. Her awareness was focused wholly on him. If only he didn't fill her field of vision. The scent of his subtle, masculine cologne teased her while the open invitation in his eyes scared her. She wasn't ready for this. More accurately, she was not prepared for the intense curiosity and desire pulsing through her. She wasn't some sex-starved adolescent. Why—and how—could this man do this to her? He moved closer, his mouth little more than a whisper from her own.

Hormones one, intellect zero.

Normally, she considered a kiss nothing more than a pleasant, harmless experience. But somewhere deep in her soul she knew kissing Matt would be as far from harmless as she could get. As his head dipped closer, she knew exactly what she should do. But when his breath caressed her face, she also knew exactly what she wanted. Him.

"My hypothesis is that you find me attractive. I'd like to test that with a kiss." There was more solicitation than insolence in his deep voice. "One kiss, DeLancey?" he asked with a touch of urgency. His tone was low and husky, and her spine seemed to dissolve, leaving her a quivering mess of desire and longing.

Their eyes locked. "I already told you, no kissing." Was that helium-high voice her own?

The smile he offered was tempered with genuine regret. That small, gallant gesture was almost enough to make her change her mind. *Remember the consequences!* her brain raged. Relationships, even brief

ones, weren't in her future. That was part of the price
she had to pay for her past.

That sobering thought gave her some much-needed
fortitude. Donning her brightest grin, she brushed his
hand from her hair, then primly folded her hands in
her lap as she faced forward. "Canfield is a two hour
drive from here," she informed him. "And that was
a pretty lame hypothesis, Professor. Want to hear
what I think it was?"

"Sure."

"My hypothesis is that it was yet another of your
adolescent attempts to kiss me."

In her peripheral vision, she saw his shrug of surrender before he fastened his seat belt and started the
engine.

"Something tells me this will be a very long two
hours," he grumbled.

"We can still take separate cars," DeLancey suggested. "You can follow—"

"I can want you and drive at the same time," Matt
retorted with a wry smile. "I'll just hang on to the
hope that you'll be so charmed by my exceptional
conversation skills you'll change your mind. That *is*
why they have those secluded rest stops along high-
ways, you know."

DeLancey laughed. "In your dreams, Professor.
Besides, I thought you wanted me to provide local
insight."

Matt drove into the throng of Sunday traffic. In
spite of the heat, summer vacationers filled the uneven sidewalks of the historic section of Charleston.

Quaint hansom cabs vied with air-conditioned buses along the more popular streets.

"Is it always like this?" Matt asked.

DeLancey nodded. "See those green flags on the lampposts?" She pointed to one. "They identify homes that are open for tours."

"Are they museums?"

"Private homes and gardens," she explained, grabbing her wind-whipped hair and holding it in a makeshift ponytail. "The historical society arranges different home tours through the year. You should check it out. The Ravanel mansion on Meeting Street is usually open."

"And I should see that because…"

"Mrs. John Ravanel, a very prominent Charleston socialite who lived there during her marriage, was murdered on Meeting Street in 1933 while walking home." She could tell by his expression that she had piqued his interest.

"The circumstances were so weird that it was days before the police even realized it was murder."

"Was she stepping out on Mr. John?" he asked.

"Mary Martin was a widow with four children. Though she had money, making a Ravanel her second husband gave her social standing. When he died, she had money and a position among the plutocrats."

"That's a big deal here?"

"It was in 1933, and it still is today. The true Charlestonians are pretty slow to accept newcomers."

"Guess that's true for Canfielders, too," Matt commented as they reached the entrance to the expressway. "Who killed her? A secret lover, perhaps? Don't all rich widows have a secret lover?"

"Do you think all murder is about sex?"

"Not all," he answered. "Just most."

DeLancey rolled her eyes. "Do you want me to tell you about poor Mary, or do you just want to talk dirty?"

He chuckled. "I want to kiss you senseless, but my mother raised me better than that. So." He sighed dramatically. "I guess I'll have to settle for the scoop on Mary."

"After the death of John Ravenel, Mary sold the mansion. She liked to gossip and entertain, not necessarily in that order."

"If she spread untruths about the other blue bloods, it's no wonder she got herself whacked."

DeLancey shifted in her seat so she could speak to him without having to yell over the noise from the open car. "This isn't some hard-boiled, dime-store detective novel, Professor. I'm trying to provide you with an accurate account of a still-unsolved crime."

"I'll behave."

"And I'll sprout wings and fly," she muttered. "Actually, Mary did say some rather racy—for the time—things. Specifically, she enjoyed sharing news of a man who lived at the corner of Meeting Street and Price's Alley. She made sure all society knew he was…not the manliest man on the face of the earth."

"Early-twentieth-century gay bashing?"

"The man was a photographer, and her rumors cost him his livelihood," DeLancey said. "But her political incorrectness isn't what makes this case so interesting.''

Matt wiggled his dark eyebrows. "The plot thickens."

"On the night of November first, Mary was taking a leisurely stroll from the Fort Sumter Hotel to her home. She was found crumpled on the sidewalk late at night, conscious but incoherent, at the corner of Meeting and Water streets. She was rushed to Roper Hospital, where she told the nurse that a man had hit her."

"Hit-and-run?"

DeLancey scoffed. "Are you sure you were a detective?"

"Yep," he answered, "Damned good one, too."

"If you say so. Anyway, she died at the hospital, and the doctor said he had examined her and found a stab wound."

"Hmm. Stabbing is a personal crime," Matt noted.

DeLancey felt a shiver dance along her spine. Was it? Had she killed someone she knew?

"Is that the end of the story?" Matt prompted.

"No." With some effort, DeLancey again pushed the past back where it belonged. "When they took her body to the funeral home, the mortician found a gunshot wound in her arm that went straight through her chest. They recovered the bullet. It was a thirty-eight, and the copper-jacketed shells were hand-filled."

"Not uncommon in the thirties," Matt suggested.

"The mayor offered a reward, but they had no clues other than the bullet."

"Sure, they did," Matt said. "Investigation protocols just weren't invented then."

"Investigation protocols?" DeLancey asked.

Matt glanced over and gave her a quick half smile. "They're like the checklist we use when investigating a homicide. With no eyewitnesses, you have to find other ways to try to discover the identity of the perp."

"Like what?"

"Like looking at the crime itself, then the victim, any trace evidence. Why?"

She shrugged and looked at her hands. "Just wondering." She thought, *Wondering if I can learn how to solve my own crime.*

"Take Mary, for instance. A gunshot implies a male perp. Men prefer guns. The scene indicates it was someone who knew her, probably knew her routine so he'd know when she'd be vulnerable."

"You can tell all that from what I've told you?"

He grinned. "If you finish the story, I can probably tell you who did it."

"Your arrogance is showing again."

"Self-assurance, DeLancey."

"Whatever. Nothing happened for three years. Then a man committed suicide in Virginia. He left a note saying he was responsible for killing Mary."

Matt shook his head. "Sounds too easy, unless he killed himself with a copper-jacketed bullet that was hand-filled."

"Shotgun," she told him, quietly impressed. "And you're correct. The police established that the man's ex-wife was part of Charleston society, and he only implicated himself in the murder to embarrass her and her family."

"What about the gay photographer?"

"The photographer left town soon after the killing, humiliated by Mary's gossip and because he had been questioned extensively by the police."

"Nothing tied him to the crime?"

"Well, almost eight years after the murder, there was a terrible storm in Charleston."

"They found the gun?" Matt deduced.

"Yes. And it still had a round in the chamber, of the same caliber and type used to kill Mary. Apparently there was a flood caused by the storm. A filing cabinet in the basement of the photographer's former home fell over, and they found the gun beneath it."

"Why didn't they search his house at the time of the murder?"

"They did."

"So did they track down the photographer and arrest him?"

DeLancey shook her head. "They sent the gun to the FBI, but it had been so damaged by salt water that they couldn't match the gun or the bullet."

Matt frowned, causing a deep furrow at his brow. "So the creep got away with it. That kind of story makes me want to scream."

"It was a long time ago," DeLancey reminded him when he pounded a fist on the steering wheel.

"Just because time passes doesn't mean a person should go unpunished."

"Maybe there were extenuating circumstances."

"And maybe some cop was smart enough to hang

onto the gun. Now the crime labs can do a whole lot more than they could in the thirties. It could be analyzed and probably yield some useful evidence.''

"Geez, Matt, if the photographer is still alive, he'd be close to one hundred."

"Then he's old enough to die in prison."

"Ever heard of compassionate justice?" DeLancey asked.

"Not when it comes to a killer."

Chapter Three

"Do you know the only thing you've said to me since we left Charleston is 'turn here' or 'turn there'?" Matt asked.

"Okay," she said, sighing. "Take Route 601 north."

"Very funny. Is something wrong?"

Even though it was midday, the effects of the sun weren't as penetrating or as harsh in the Olde English District. This part of South Carolina was very different from the low country of the Charleston area.

"Nothing. I've just been taking in the scenery."

"It's very pretty up here. But are you sure we're close to civilization?"

"Ha, ha. Canfield is a community of less than a thousand people."

"You're joking, I hope."

She couldn't stifle her grin. "Nope. And on Sundays, we have supper around four, then roll up the streets for the night."

"No nightlife?"

"In Camden," she explained. "But that's another forty-eight miles of hilly, winding roads."

"No wonder you moved away."

"I moved away to work," DeLancey responded. "If Canfield could sustain a restaurant, I'd be back here in a flash."

As she finished her sentence, Matt slowed to the posted speed. She didn't think he'd be too impressed if she told him he had just passed the only speed-limit sign in Canfield.

They entered the small town the only way possible—down the main street. Canfield consisted of a single street with small shops, a town square, three churches, a library and a school complex that served kindergarten through grade twelve. Matt downshifted as they came to the center of town. "It looks like Mayberry."

DeLancey grinned. "Then you must be Goober."

He turned his head to playfully sneer at her. The action caused a lock of his raven hair to fall forward. DeLancey reached out to fix it, realized what she was about to do and snapped her hand away as if she'd reached for fire.

His faux sneer turned into a purely lecherous grin. "You have an open invitation to touch me."

"I'll keep that in mind," she retorted as a loud horn sounded from behind them. DeLancey turned and saw Miss Foster, Canfield's answer to Mae West, behind the wheel of her 1950-something pickup. She waved and smiled.

Miss Foster thrust her head out of the window and

called, "'Bout time you brought a young man home."

DeLancey yelled back, "I'm not keeping him, so don't you go starting any stories. He's just an acquaintance."

"Then bring him down to my place, child. If you don't want him, I sure do. He's a cute one."

"Only from a distance!" DeLancey called as she shoved Matt's shoulder. "Drive, would you?" she asked urgently.

"And run the risk of offending Ma Kettle?"

"No making fun of the locals, and stop turning around to smile at the woman. She spreads rumors faster than bacteria can multiply. Just drive."

Grinning, Matt complied, but only after giving Miss Foster an outrageous wink and a wave. "Friendly place."

"Miss Foster likes to shock and tease people. She's probably in her eighties. Her come-ons are her attempt to scandalize and nothing but talk, so try not to let it go to your already inflated head."

In less than a minute, they were through town proper. The car passed under a canopy of live oaks draped with gray moss. They continued down a road, which became more narrow and less well groomed.

"Are there any archivists in town?"

DeLancey chuckled. "The widow Cooper is the librarian, Sunday school teacher and the town notary. She goes into the county seat once a month to record deeds and other documents."

"At least Mayberry had a courthouse," Matt grumbled. "I thought Shelby said you researched old murders as a hobby. Where did you get your information?''

Inwardly, DeLancey shivered. ''It's not a hobby, really.''

He took his eyes off the road to give her a sidelong glance. ''What is it, then?''

She shrugged. ''It's an interest, period. What about you? Why aren't you in law school?''

''Huh?''

''I thought all disillusioned cops went to law school.''

He smiled, blew on his fingertips and rubbed them on his shirt. ''What can I say? I'm unique.''

She sighed loudly. ''So much for meaningful conversation.''

''I was joking, DeLancey. Lighten up. I opted to study criminal justice from a different perspective.''

More intrigued than she would care to admit, even to herself, she asked, ''Why?''

''I spent a good deal of my early career working my tail off putting scum behind bars, only to rearrest them a week, a month, a year later. As far as I'm concerned, that means the system doesn't work.''

''Aren't you supposed to make changes from within?'' DeLancey asked. ''Why not stay on the force and try—''

''It wasn't an option.''

The forcefulness and suddenness of his remark caught her off guard. ''Why not?''

His face hardened. ''I screwed up a case. There's no room for mistakes when lives are at stake.''

DeLancey felt a twinge of compassion for him. "What happened?"

"Nothing worth talking about," he insisted. It seemed to take him under a minute to recover. His jaw muscles relaxed, and it wasn't long before his charming, dimpled smile was securely in place. "How many more years are we going to be on this back road?"

"I guess that's my cue to drop the subject?" she asked. "The Tillman Plantation is about four miles ahead on the right."

Matt flexed his fingers against the steering wheel, hoping the monotony of the action would dissipate some of the tension that had come with her innocent question regarding his departure from the NYPD. He had enough trouble keeping the memory of Jenny's lifeless eyes out of his dreams. He sure didn't want it to become part of his consciousness again. Matt slowed the car when he spotted an old wrought-iron gate with elaborate carvings guarding a gravel driveway. The initials *T* and *P* served as finials at each side of the gate.

DeLancey called, "Hold on!" leaped from the car and began jogging toward the closed gate.

The only thing Matt wanted to hold on to was her. As he watched her long-legged lope, he was again taken by her natural beauty. Her face glowed with almost childlike happiness as she bent to do battle with an ancient latch.

Beams of sunlight painted amber highlights in her dark hair. Matt knew he should get out of the car and offer to help, but he guessed she would consider such a show of chivalry an insult. Instead, he used his position to openly ogle the woman. He hated himself for thinking such thoughts, but he liked the view too much to look away. Though every inch of her incredible body exuded femininity, DeLancey wasn't frail or fragile. Quite the contrary, he thought as he watched her push the right side of the gate open. Her olive complexion glistened with a touch of perspiration. Wiping her hands on the front of her shorts, she jogged to the car with the enthusiasm of a child about to enter the gates of Disney World.

He stared at her for a minute, completely caught up in her apparent joy at returning home. With her hair mussed from the trip and her lips slightly parted as she took deep breaths, she was absolutely glorious. What Matt couldn't figure out was why this woman, who clearly had no use for him, was fast becoming the obsession of his fantasies.

"Drive!" she urged, sliding into the seat beside him.

Matt smiled and threw the car in gear. The parched dirt road erupted in clouds of reddish brown dust. Gnarled old trees lined the drive, guarding the battered road like a row of attentive soldiers. He drove nearly a half mile before an assortment of buildings came into view.

"This is an estate?" he asked after surveying the wooden shells that were probably barns and stables in their heyday. Now they were little more than skeletons with caved-in roofs. A house stood in the center of the dilapidated outbuildings. In his judgment, it was in only slightly better shape than the rest.

"It was," she answered with a touch of defensiveness. "In the 1820s, this was the largest farm in the county. The Tillmans are Canfield's version of royalty." Matt stopped the car at the foot of a set of marble steps that were chipped and markedly slanting to the left. He lifted his sunglasses, thinking the place might look better if it wasn't viewed through dark lenses. He was wrong.

DeLancey raced from the car. She took the steps two at a time. Just as she reached the top, one of the mahogany doors opened.

The man who stepped out to greet her looked more like a lumberjack than royalty. His face was almost obscured by a scruffy beard. A hat with the insignia of some tractor company veiled his eyes. He wrapped big, beefy arms around DeLancey and twirled her off the ground. Her laughter filled the dusty air, causing a strange tightness in Matt's gut. It didn't take a rocket scientist to know what he was feeling. Jealousy, plain and simple. He would love to get such a warm hug from the aloof DeLancey. Barring that, he'd settle for an opportunity to hold her against him.

The love fest between the lumberjack and DeLancey came to an end as Matt climbed the stairs with the cooler perched on one shoulder.

"Matt Tanner," he said, offering the man his hand.

"Joe Gomez," the man said as his light eyes quietly communicated a fair amount of distrust and disapproval.

"Joe," Matt acknowledged. Apparently he wasn't the only one who felt an innate need to protect DeLancey.

"Gomez." The man grumbled the correction. Then, abruptly, he turned to DeLancey. The small portion of his face that wasn't covered with bushy hair in three different colors, the most predominant of which was gray, showed genuine concern. "She's in a bad way."

DeLancey responded by abandoning the two of them and racing into the house.

"I'll show you to the kitchen," Gomez said, then turned on the heel of his worn work boots.

Stepping inside the house was like stepping back in time. Though just about everything was layered with a healthy coat of dust, Matt knew enough about antiques to recognize several quality pieces in the grand foyer.

He followed Gomez down the dark hallway to the back of the house.

"Looks like Bob Vila has been here," he joked.

Gomez, his expression completely devoid of humor, met his gaze. "Mrs. P. did this when DeLancey showed a hankering for cooking."

"Nice," Matt said as he ran his hand over the cool marble countertop. The state-of-the-art kitchen included every gadget and gizmo he'd ever seen and a few he hadn't. "She must have loved it."

"Still does," Gomez answered, softening a bit. "Every time she comes for a visit, she practices on us."

Matt smiled. "I've tasted her food at the Rose Tattoo. She's a great chef."

"That she is," Gomez agreed. "Mrs. P. was a fine cook in her day. I think DeLancey got some of her talent that way. When she was a young thing, her and Mrs. P. used to spend hours cooking and baking. They'd send me out to the neighbors with the food. It helped a lot of folks who needed it.''

Matt flipped open the cooler and started placing things in the nearly bare refrigerator. ''Mrs. Pembleton sounds like a wonderful woman. How are she and DeLancey related?''

Gomez adjusted his cap, tipped the bill and walked out a rickety screen door without another word.

Matt finished putting things in the refrigerator. Since Gomez had abandoned him and DeLancey was somewhere in the huge house tending to the ailing owner, he decided to give himself a tour of the first floor.

It felt good to walk after the long drive, even if the old pine-plank floor creaked in protest with his every step. The walls were expertly carved mahogany from floor to ceiling. It made the house feel dark and mysterious. *Or maybe I'm just bored and my mind is working overtime,* he thought with a sigh.

The first door he opened was a closet. Several coats hung neatly on a sagging rod. There was a musty odor, as if he was the first person in this century to open the door.

Moving on, he found a dining room that looked as if it hadn't been used in a few decades. There was a living room with small Victorian sofas and game tables. Doilies on the furniture had long since yellowed, as had some of the paintings on the walls. He went toward an ornate fireplace to get a better look at the portraits hanging above the mantel. By the style of clothing and hair depicted, he guessed them to date from the late thirties, maybe early forties. The first was of a woman, striking in a red ball gown. Her hands were clasped in her lap. The artist had captured the sparkle of a huge diamond on the fourth finger of her left hand. The other painting was of a stiff but handsome-looking gentleman dressed in morning clothes. The quality of the paintings was noteworthy.

"She was beautiful then, wasn't she?"

Matt turned and found DeLancey in the doorway, her big eyes red and full of sadness. "You okay?" he asked her.

She shrugged. "It's hard to see her like this. Mrs. Pembleton was always a strong, independent woman. Now she's as weak as a bird, and she's so thin."

Matt acted on instinct. He moved to her, gathering her in his arms and pulling her against him. Gently, he stroked her hair as she cried softly.

When her sobs had evolved into little more than sniffles, DeLancey stepped out of his embrace. She wiped her eyes, then raked her fingers through her hair. "Sorry."

"What for?" he asked, placing his finger beneath her chin and forcing her to look at him.

She gave a little forced laugh. "Because I find it a tad humiliating to weep openly in front of a virtual stranger."

It was his turn to laugh. "You're being weird. There's no crime in crying."

"Right, it accomplishes so much," she murmured. "I'm going to go start dinner."

"Wait," he said, and grasped her arm. "Isn't cooking something of a busman's holiday for you?"

She shook her head. "Cooking is therapy for me."

Matt shrugged and let her go. He knew firsthand that throwing oneself into an absorbing task could help take one's mind off things. Wasn't he doing the same thing?

He followed her into the kitchen, struck again by how out of place the kitchen looked in the deteriorating house. Grabbing a stool, he parked himself across from her at the kitchen island. He told himself he was watching her for the noblest of reasons. If DeLancey was going to fall apart again, he wanted to be there to offer comfort. However, when he saw the effect of her culinary endeavor on her rosy cheeks and sparkling eyes, his motives took a definite detour.

"This place could use some TLC."

She smiled. "Don't mince words, Professor. This house is falling down."

"Why not fix it up? There's some great architecture here, as well as some valuable antiques."

The hand wielding the knife stopped in midchop. "Casing the joint?" she teased.

Matt grabbed a slice of green pepper and popped it into his mouth. "I did a little investigating."

"I guess it will be up to Alan to fix it up or tear it down and sell the land parcel by parcel."

"Alan?"

"Faircloth," she answered, tossing him another slice of pepper. "He's Mrs. P.'s only living relative."

Matt felt his brow fold as he frowned. "So why isn't he over here taking care of her?"

"He does what he can," DeLancey said with a hint of censure. "He's a lawyer. He has offices in Canfield and Columbia." She placed the sliced peppers to one side, went to the refrigerator and retrieved an armload of ingredients. "He'll be here for dinner."

"Why?"

"Alan likes good food, especially when he doesn't have to pay for it."

"You aren't painting a very pleasant picture of the guy. Why make him dinner?"

"I need him."

"For what?"

She met his eyes. "To help me convince Mrs. P. to let Dr. Howard come."

"Why doesn't she want to see a doctor?"

"She's in her seventies. She's stubborn. And she's never really liked Dr. Howard examining her, since he's an old family friend. Take your pick."

"How long has she been sick?"

"About two months, on and off."

"What are her symptoms?"

"It started with stomach pains. Then dizziness and weakness. She's freezing. Now she's nauseous all the time and can barely keep food down."

"Sounds serious," Matt acknowledged.

"It's probably some form of cancer. Maybe there's still enough time to get treatment."

"There's always hope."

His comment earned him one of her rare smiles.

"You aren't such a bad guy, after all."

He winked. "Told you so."

Her expression grew somber. "Look. It would be

a lot easier for us to be friends if I didn't feel like you were the hunter and I was the prey.''

"I don't hunt. Don't believe in it. Now, football, that's a true sport.''

"You want to talk sports?'' DeLancey rolled her eyes. "I'm trying to define our relationship.''

Matt couldn't hide his smile. "So, we're going to have a relationship, after all?''

That remark earned him a stern, silent rebuke.

Clearing his throat, he humbly said, "Sorry.''

"I can't offer you anything more than friendship.''

"Can't or won't?''

"What's the difference? Besides, the result is the same. I've got too much stuff in my life to complicate it by being some temporary toy for a man who has a full life, an exciting career and whatever else in another part of the country.''

Matt let out a low whistle. "Sounds like I've been tried and convicted in absentia.''

"Meaning?''

Matt was growing irritated. "You've decided that I use women as temporary toys. I don't think you know me well enough to make that kind of a generalization.''

She looked at him with narrowed eyes. "I know leering. I know innuendo.''

"Try appreciative glances and an effort to communicate my genuine interest.''

She looked away. "This is getting us nowhere.''

"Not in my opinion.''

"Look, I'm not at my best at the moment. Can we

have this argument later? Right now I could really use some breathing room.''

Matt rose, went to the refrigerator and grabbed one of the bottles of wine he'd unpacked. As he stalked from the kitchen, he took a glass almost as an after-thought. He felt a little like a child storming out of the room, but her unflattering assessment of his motivation and his character stung.

He stepped onto a shaded porch and settled himself on a wooden swing. Using his Swiss Army knife, Matt removed the cork and poured a healthy amount of the wine into the glass. He began to let go of his anger as he scanned the landscape. If someone took the time to repair the fences and clear away the rusting farm machinery, the view would be incredible. In the distance, he saw Gomez pushing a lawnmower. Given the size of the land, it was kind of like trying to drain a river with an eyedropper.

As the sun dropped lower, so did Matt's spirits. Maybe he'd played this all wrong. ''A temporary toy,'' he muttered. Sure, he was attracted enough to pursue DeLancey, but he'd never considered her as a vacation fling.

''So what *were* you thinking?'' he asked himself. For some reason, all day he'd found himself remembering his life in New York, his partner, Scott...and Scott's wife, Jenny. Although they were physically very different, something about DeLancey reminded Matt of Jenny. Some sort of vulnerability, a kind of appeal in their eyes.

Jenny. Just thinking the name, as always, twisted Matt's gut with regret. If only he had paid more attention to his partner's increasing fits of temper. With a naiveté that now seemed incredible to him, Matt had chalked up the slow decline in dinner invitations as a result of their long work hours. He'd dismissed that one time he'd dropped by and Jenny had refused to let him inside, claiming a migraine as she hid behind the door. Somehow he'd missed the obvious— his partner, Scott, the all-American good guy, had been beating his wife for years. There was no getting around the fact that Matt's lack of attention had played a role in Jenny's death. Matt knew he would spend the rest of his life wondering if he could have done more had he realized sooner. Never again would he allow himself to care about someone without knowing all about them. Never again would he believe the face a person presented to the world was their true face. If that made him suspicious, so be it.

DeLancey was wrong about his life in New York. There was nothing there for him anymore. Not since Jenny.

Chapter Four

"Hormones one, intellect one," she whispered as she continued to prepare dinner. "I should be happy. Now Matt knows where I stand."

All Matt knows is that you came off like a nasty shrew, she thought as her frustration added speed and intensity to the wire whisk in her hand. The egg whites reached the stiff-peak stage in record time.

Once the mocha mousse was in the freezer, she couldn't think of anything keeping her from admitting to Matt that she might have come on a little strong. So she went in search of him.

She found him lounging on the porch swing. His long legs were stretched out in front of him, crossed at the ankles. The minute the screen door closed behind her, he looked up.

She watched the play of emotion in his eyes. She saw caution and confusion and felt another pang of guilt. After all, Matt had never done anything to her but be kind, even if his kindness was peppered with some outrageous remarks.

Mustering her courage, she said, "I was way out of line before."

"Yes, you were."

Tilting her head, she tried to read his blank expression. "Although—you *have* been coming on pretty strong."

Matt didn't respond.

"I was trying to make the point that my life is…well, I just don't have time for complications."

Matt still didn't respond.

DeLancey threw her arms up, then let them slap against her thighs. "I'm sorry! What more do you want?"

Matt grinned. "That was all I wanted."

"To have me grovel?"

He stood and came to her. His finger touched her chin. She felt the warmth of his gentle touch. He urged her face up until she had no choice but to look deeply into his gaze. A flame seemed to ignite in the pit of her stomach. The heat spread through her from the inside. She hoped the sensation was a result of her embarrassment and not a response to his slightest touch.

Matt's thumb began a light, gentle stroking of her cheek as he looked at her with kindness and sincerity.

"I didn't want you to grovel."

"They why did you make me?"

"I didn't *make* you do anything."

Right, like you aren't making my knees weak right this instant. "You didn't acknowledge my apology."

"You didn't apologize right away," he said as his thumb trailed ever closer to her mouth.

DeLancey opened her mouth, but it was several seconds before any sound came out. "I did, too."

He kept staring into her eyes as his other hand went behind her to rest on her shoulder blade.

Hormones two, intellect one, she admitted as she willingly moved against his solid body. Standing there in the warm glow of dusk was purely and totally intoxicating. As his fingers explored the valley of her spine, DeLancey decided it wouldn't be the end of the world if she tested the waters. Besides, she reasoned, she was tired and drained. Mrs. P. was in terrible shape. The Rose Tattoo was shut down for renovations. What was the harm in accepting from Matt the comfort he seemed so very willing to give?

Tentatively, she placed her hands at his waistband. She felt him flinch at her touch, which made her wonder if she had read his intentions correctly. Then he dispelled all her fears by pulling her closer. DeLancey was fascinated by the raw strength beneath the expensive clothes. Everywhere she touched she felt hard, corded muscle. It was like being in that silly commercial where the granite statue of a god comes to luscious life.

While she was making her own explorations, Matt's hand slipped beneath her hair to caress the sensitive skin at the nape of her neck. His gray eyes darkened and smoldered as he dropped his gaze when he cupped her face in his palms. Warm, wine-scented breath washed over her flushed face. Matt guided her slowly, so that her face was in a perfect position to receive his kiss.

Kiss. DeLancey blinked. *Where is my brain?* she screamed to her passion-dulled senses. Bracing her hands against his muscled torso, she pushed out of his arms. She stepped away until she felt the railing against her back. At least she could lean there until the muscles in her legs stopped quivering. It wasn't her legs, really. Her entire body was quivering. And, she had to admit, there was more. She wasn't just overcome by a moment of lust. Her heart was racing, apparently trying to catch up to the thoughts dashing through her mind. This wasn't lust. This was something more. Something scary and powerful. Something she absolutely didn't want to deal with. ''I—I don't know what came over me,'' she stammered. ''I only came out here to apologize to you.''

Matt flashed his dimples. ''If that's how you do it, you're welcome to apologize to me anytime.''

DeLancey felt her face flame. ''You're making this worse,'' she groused.

''That was the idea.'' Matt extended his hand.

DeLancey glared at it like he was offering up an angry cobra. ''Don't touch me.''

''I was simply going to escort you inside.''

''Why? I told you it was a mistake. I'm sure not going to take your hand so we can continue this inside.''

Matt's smile never wavered. ''I heard a car, so I

assume that your dinner guest is here. I was offering to see you inside, not see you naked, though…''

"Stop!" Her blush got worse.

She didn't take his hand, nor did she react when he placed his hand on her back as he ushered her inside. "I didn't hear the car. You must have great ears."

Matt waited until they were one step from the front door before he leaned next to her ear and whispered, "By the way, it wasn't a mistake, DeLancey. It was magic."

She was sure she looked like a guilty adolescent when she opened the door to greet Alan. Guilt was replaced by genuine surprise when she saw a younger man teetering on the step just behind the attorney.

"Nice to see you, DeLancey," Alan said as he bent and kissed the air in her general direction.

"You, too, Alan." She stepped aside. "I'd like you to meet Professor Matthew Tanner."

Alan's eyebrows arched, making it unnecessary for him to vocalize his thoughts. Of course, DeLancey could hardly blame him for thinking Matt was her lover. She probably looked all hot and bothered. Because she was.

"Professor," Alan said. "I'm Esther Pembleton's attorney in addition to being her cousin. Twice removed on my mother's side."

Matt smiled.

"Allow me to introduce my associate, Stephen Thomason. Stephen recently joined my firm."

DeLancey smiled at the attractive man who seemed much friendlier and a lot less pretentious than Alan. Stephen looked like he had stepped off the cover of a businessman's journal. His suit was conservative, his tie fashionable and his manners impeccable. His fair hair, blue eyes and perfect white teeth screamed Ivy League. "Miss Jones, I've heard wonderful things about you," he said, gushing. "Alan tells me your culinary skills are unsurpassed around here."

DeLancey gave him a modest smile. "Since the only restaurant in Canfield is Halloway's Luncheonette, it isn't hard to do better than a greasy omelette or a bowl of overcooked greens."

Stephen's blue eyes twinkled with amusement, and DeLancey became aware of two things. First, Stephen still held her hand. Second, Matt was staring at the two men as if they were suspects in some major crime.

"I'm glad you could join us," DeLancey said. Turning to Alan, she added, "I hope there's enough."

Alan brushed off her small dig with a wave of his manicured hand. "You always make enough for an army. Besides, Stephen and Esther have become quite close these past few months."

"How nice," DeLancey said as the two new arrivals entered the house.

Before she could follow, Matt grabbed her arm and whispered, "How convenient."

"What?"

"Thomason made friends with Mrs. Pembleton at about the same time she became ill?"

DeLancey shrugged his suspicions off. "You're not very trusting, are you?"

"Better than being too trusting," he retorted.

"I'm certainly not that," DeLancey insisted. "If anything, I find it hard to trust."

"Is that why you didn't want me to kiss you?"

DeLancey let out a slow breath and closed her eyes. "I've got to get supper together. Do we have to discuss this now?"

Matt shook his head. "It can wait…a little while."

"I knew letting you tag along was going to be a problem." She sighed as she started down the hall with Matt close behind. "I can call the truck stop and see if there are any rooms available."

"Pass, thanks."

"Then be nice," she admonished. "Remember, I'm a squatter here. It's Alan who is family."

Matt followed her into the kitchen where Faircloth and his young, eager associate were pouring themselves glasses of wine. Matt studied them. Thomason was easy to read. He was a young, hungry lawyer who was probably hoping to inherit Faircloth's practice some day. Faircloth was a little more complex. His dated seersucker suit gave him a clichéd simple-country-lawyer look. However, he seemed to have both a sharp mind and a subtle cruelty in his eyes. Surely a bright woman like DeLancey could see through Faircloth's persona.

"What brings you to Canfield?" Faircloth asked as he took a seat at the head of the long table in the dining room, just off the kitchen. He made something of a production out of rearranging the long strands of thin, graying hair at the sides of his head. Apparently he thought that by growing enough hair to comb over his bald spot, no one would notice he had fewer than fifty hairs to his name.

"I'm on sabbatical from Glens Falls College in up-state New York."

"Tanner? Are you any relation to that darling young woman who employs our DeLancey?" he drawled.

"Shelby is my sister-in-law."

Faircloth nodded, as did Thomason, making the two appear mirror images. Maybe they were. Maybe Stephen was a suave, cultured version of Faircloth.

"Lovely woman, Mrs. Tanner. To me she embodies all that we hold dear here in the South."

DeLancey gave Matt a glass of wine when she brought her own. "Supper will be ready in a little while." She went to the refrigerator and returned with a tray of appetizers that looked too good to eat. "I hope you like shrimp, Mr. Thomason."

"I'm looking forward to a sampling," Thomason answered.

Even if DeLancey couldn't see it, Matt thought, Stephen's tone made it clear he was referring to her and not to the shrimp wrapped in phyllo.

"Some people are allergic," DeLancey said as she took the seat between the young attorney and Matt.

"Anything that looks this good can't possibly be bad for you."

Thomason spoke directly to DeLancey's chest. Matt felt ready to explode. "Do you need any help in the kitchen?" Matt asked her.

DeLancey gave him a brush-off smile. "Everything is under control." She turned to Thomason. "When did you go to work for Alan, Mr. Thomason?"

"Call me Stephen," he said, almost purring.

Matt couldn't decide what made him more ill—the man's unctuous tones and flirtatious manner or the fact that DeLancey didn't seem to mind them.

"What brings you to South Carolina, Mr. Tanner?" Faircloth asked.

"Research. I'm finishing my doctorate and hope to get it published."

"How interesting. In what field, if I may be so inquisitive?"

Since his other option was watching Thomason simper over DeLancey, Matt decided dull small talk with the elder attorney was the lesser evil. "Criminal justice."

Faircloth smiled. "An element of our society with which I am—regrettably—somewhat familiar."

"I'm focusing on unsolved cases. Know of any in the area?"

Faircloth stroked the upper of his two chins. "Not

that I can recall this minute. But I'll be glad to have one of my paralegals look into the matter.''

Matt nodded and lifted his glass. ''That would be very helpful, thanks.''

Faircloth's smile didn't reach his eyes. ''We always like to assist out-of-town guests.''

''Get many of them around here?''

Faircloth scoffed. ''In Canfield? I do believe our DeLancey was the last person to move to Canfield. Since they built the interstate, folks just pass on by.''

''It wasn't the easiest place to find. Without De-Lancey's directions, I probably would have blinked and missed the place. No offense,'' Matt added, belatedly remembering he was maligning the man's hometown.

''None taken. Esther is my only real tie to Canfield these days. I do maintain an office here, but more out of nostalgia than necessity. Most of my work is in Columbia.''

''Speaking of Mrs. P.,'' DeLancey interjected, ''she's really not well, Alan. You've got to convince her to see Dr. Howard.''

''I'm quite aware that Cousin Esther is ailing, DeLancey. I've tried to broach the subject with her on numerous occasions. Half the time I call, that rude hired man she keeps around won't even put the call through. Arrogant old goat.''

''Gomez isn't arrogant.'' DeLancey defended him hotly. ''He loves Mrs. Pembleton. He's just very protective.''

Matt had a suspicion it wasn't the first time De-Lancey and the heir to the crumbling throne had covered this territory.

"He does seem cooperative—if a little odd," Stephen suggested in a blatant attempt to score points with DeLancey.

What a ferret, Matt thought with disgust.

"After supper, Stephen and I will take a tray up to Esther. Perhaps between the two of us, we can convince her to let us call a physician. Or better yet, get her into a nice assisted-living facility in Columbia."

Matt watched the color drain from DeLancey's face. "You know she doesn't want that, Alan. She's always said that she wants to stay in this house until the last breath leaves her body."

Faircloth gave her a patronizing look. "She isn't safe here. This house is a death trap."

"Gomez looks after the house," DeLancey argued. "It may not be in all its original glory, but he's always made sure that the east wing is structurally sound."

"The stairs are dangerous. Leaving her here is like asking for a serious accident."

"She hasn't left her room in weeks, Alan. I hardly think we have to worry about her taking a header down the steps."

"There's no need for sarcasm, young lady. I'll speak to Esther. If she continues to refuse treatment, I'll have no choice but to exercise my power of attorney and force her to take proper care of herself."

"I wasn't being sarcastic," DeLancey said in a subdued tone. "It's just that I hate seeing her in such discomfort. I'm really worried."

"As am I," Faircloth insisted. "After all, she is my closest relative."

"I'll get the food on the table."

"I'll help," Matt said. He felt a childish satisfaction that he'd been faster to offer help than the ferret. Stifling the urge to give in completely to this immaturity and offer his tongue to the other man, Matt followed DeLancey into the next room. "Interesting duo."

She rolled her eyes. "Alan is a pompous jerk. But Mrs. P. does listen to him. And that Thomason guy is something else."

"He was all but drooling over you."

She grinned. "Sickening, wasn't it?"

"So why didn't you tell him to take a hike?"

"You heard Alan. He said Mrs. P. likes him. I didn't want to jeopardize offending him if he can help."

Matt reached around her and lifted a lid off a pot. "How about if I jeopardize him?"

She giggled. "Like you're any better than he, Professor. If you were any closer right now, we'd be sharing skin cells."

"I'm only trying to help."

"Then help another way." She slipped beneath his arm. "Stir that while I get everything together."

Matt obediently did as she asked. Every now and

then he would turn, either to catch a glimpse of DeLancey or to watch the two men in the other room. Faircloth and the ferret seemed to be involved in a rather animated, whispered conversation. And something told Matt that Faircloth wasn't giving the ferret a friendly warning to stay away from DeLancey. They were clearly a team.

DeLancey's incredible meal received thanks from Faircloth and a continued rain of unimaginative come-ons from Thomason. However, the dinner did yield some progress as far as Matt was concerned. Every time Thomason or Faircloth said something particularly pretentious or stupid, he'd glance across the table to meet DeLancey's laughing eyes. Their shared secret amusement reminded him of the silent communication he had often had with his siblings. Maybe he was making some headway. Or did that mean she had sisterly feelings for him?

Matt did the dishes after a brief battle with De-Lancey. Faircloth and Thomason had brandy and lit smelly cigars. At Matt's urging, DeLancey went out on the porch to relax with a glass of wine.

When Matt was finished, he joined her, happy to get away from the acrid smoke. She'd kicked off her sandals and tucked her legs beneath her, making her look small and vulnerable. She seemed to be staring at the stars.

"Is this seat taken?"

The smile she offered was wistful, pensive. "It's a free swing."

He sat beside her, breathing in the fresh scent of her subtle perfume. It was a welcome change from the cigar smoke, not to mention just faint enough to be incredibly sensuous. "What are you thinking about?"

"Stuff."

"Want me to point out the constellations for you?"

"Nope."

"Good, since my knowledge of the vast cosmos begins and ends with the Big Dipper."

She laughed. "Then what would you have done if I'd said yes?"

"Lied."

"That's comforting, Professor. Do most women fall for your charms even though they are complete baloney?"

"Most women fall for my good looks, or so I've been told."

"Geez, humble, aren't you?"

"It was a joke, DeLancey. Incidentally—" he lowered his voice "—I can't say I have a high opinion of your cousin Alan."

"He isn't my cousin."

Matt shrugged. "Great-uncle twice removed, or whatever he is."

"He's nothing to me. Mrs. P. isn't a relative—she just took me in when I was fifteen."

"So that's what you meant when you said you were a squatter here?"

"Yes. She's been wonderful to me, but I've always known it was temporary."

He nudged her with his shoulder. "Temporary? You make it sound like you grew up with your suitcase packed and ready under the bed."

She sighed. "It's complicated."

The conversation was interrupted when they heard footsteps going upstairs. "I guess Cousin Alan is about to do his family duty."

"Let's hope. I'll drag Dr. Howard out here without her permission and move in to nurse her full-time before I'll let Alan put her in some assisted-living place."

"From what you've said, I think that's the right thing to do."

"It may be right, but I'll still have to fight Alan over this house. He's got total control of Mrs. P.'s meager funds, and I don't have enough saved to keep this place up and take care of her properly."

"What about health insurance? Won't it pay for someone to come in?"

"Maybe," she answered. "I'll look into it if Alan tries to take her out of here."

Matt placed his arm around DeLancey, and she allowed her head to rest against his shoulder. Silently, he said a little prayer of thanks that his parents were still healthy and vital. With the cares on her shoulders, DeLancey seemed like the oldest twenty-five-year-old he'd ever met.

Thomason appeared first, skidding through the

screen door, followed by the lumbering Faircloth. The older attorney looked at DeLancey and spoke calmly as if he was delivering the latest weather.

"I've called for the paramedics. Cousin Esther is unresponsive."

DeLancey clung to Matt as they stood up. "What do you mean unresponsive?"

Chapter Five

Matt stood mutely as an elderly doctor emerged from the trauma room. His shock of white hair was mussed, probably from removing the green cap that dangled from one hand.

He walked to where they stood in a loosely fashioned semicircle. When he lifted his eyes, it was to look directly at DeLancey. Hanging his head, he softly said, "I'm sorry."

DeLancey let out a plaintive wail. It was a sound Matt was familiar with from his police days, so he was ready when she collapsed. Standing behind her, Matt wrapped his arms around her. Grasping her flailing wrists, he lifted her and held on. DeLancey's small body shook as she sobbed uncontrollably.

"HOW IS SHE?" Matt asked when the doctor came downstairs. They'd come back to the plantation an hour or two ago.

"I've sedated her. She was exhausted, but too upset to sleep."

"Want one?" Matt asked, pointing at the bottle of brandy he'd discovered in one of the cabinets.

The doctor smiled. "I guess I'm off-duty now." Accepting a glass, he fell into the chair across from Matt as though he, too, were on the brink of exhaustion. As Dr. Howard cradled the snifter in both hands, Matt noted that his graceful surgeon's fingers were crooked from age.

"Are you and DeLancey...close?" the doctor inquired.

"Not really. Not that I'm not trying."

Howard smiled. "She's not the kind of girl to let people get close. Never was."

Matt's interest was piqued. "You've known her long?"

The doctor's expression was blank. "Since she arrived here," he said carefully.

"When was that?" Matt pursued.

Howard took a fortifying swallow of the brandy. "Ten years ago, give or take."

"Where did she come from?"

Howard reached into a pocket in his vest, retrieved a pocket watch, flipped open the hunter-style case, then let out a breath. "I appreciate the drink, Mr. Tanner. I've got to get going." He finished his brandy in one long sip, then went to where he had left his medical bag on the counter and pulled out a sample bottle of pills and a business card. "When she wakes up, give her one of these every four hours. Feel free to call me if you have any questions or concerns."

Matt had plenty of both. After placing the glasses in the sink, he quietly moved through the house. A carved staircase led him to the second floor. Mindful of the sleeping DeLancey, he tried to move silently, but no matter how softly he trod, the old timbers creaked loudly with each step.

The upper floor was a good ten degrees warmer and completely silent. He walked slowly, taking in the small antique side tables and the old paintings that lined the hallway. Since Joe Gomez had insisted on carrying DeLancey upstairs when they returned to the house, Matt wasn't sure which room she was in.

He went to the first door he saw and gingerly pushed against it. It opened into a small, dark room. Taking a step inside, he fumbled for the light switch. A single fixture on the ceiling came to life after a few flickers. Matt's attention went to the rumpled bed-sheets. The scent of stale food mixed with a strong floral scent.

The food smell came from a tray on the edge of a dresser. The floral smell was from an overturned perfume bottle next to the tray. Moving closer, he found a series of framed photographs and news clippings on the large bedside table. Lifting one, he blew away a layer of dust and looked at DeLancey's image. Whoever took the photograph had captured a smile that reached her eyes. He guessed the photograph was five or six years old. Matt knew it had been taken here because he recognized the porch in the background of the photo. Using the pad of his index finger, Matt traced the devilish curve of her mouth. He set down the frame, and turned to the next one.

DeLancey had won some sort of culinary award. A picture showed her decked out in her chef's whites, grinning as she held the gold medallion around her neck toward the camera.

Since he knew Faircloth and the ferret had taken a tray to Mrs. Pembleton, he knew he must be standing in the woman's bedroom. From the plethora of mementos, Matt also knew that Mrs. Pembleton had loved DeLancey dearly. Judging by the way DeLancey had collapsed at the hospital, the feeling was mutual. She'd hate to see the room looking like this, so empty and abandoned. Matt decided that after he checked on DeLancey, he would return to tidy up the bedroom.

As he replaced the frame, he noticed a faint but distinct outline on the tabletop. It was rectangular, the exact dimensions of an envelope. There was also a disturbance in the dust behind the last photograph. Matt ran his finger inside the outlines. It came away clean. Whatever items had been there had only recently been removed.

Matt continued his search for DeLancey. There were several more rooms, mostly filled with boxes, furniture and piles of old magazines. Apparently Mrs. Pembleton was something of a pack rat. He found DeLancey in the last room on the left.

She was in an old four-poster bed, curled in a fetal position. DeLancey didn't stir as he moved toward her. With the exception of some puffiness around her eyes, she looked peaceful and snug with the coverlet pulled up to her shoulder. He watched the rhythmic rise and fall of the blanket as she breathed deeply and evenly. When he reached out to brush a few strands of hair off her face, Matt felt a pang of guilt.

Using the back of his hand, he gently stroked the hollow of her cheek. He knew full well she probably wouldn't tolerate such an action if she was awake. Still, he felt powerless to stop. It was mesmerizing to caress her skin, to feel her breath spill over his hand. He felt a tightness in the pit of his stomach. The knot was partly a result of his unconditional desire to see her through her pain. The other part was knowing with near certainty that she would never return his feelings.

"HOW IS SHE?"

"Still sleeping," Matt told Gomez. The man had slipped silently into the kitchen. "Want some coffee?"

Gomez studied him for a few seconds before giving a slight nod. He stood framed in the doorway and watched as Matt got a cup and poured coffee from the pot. "How do you take it?"

"Black's fine."

Matt placed the cup on the countertop in front of the uncommunicative man. With his face virtually covered with scraggly hair and his eyes shrouded in the shadow from the bill of his hat, Gomez looked like a film noir informant.

"DeLancey brought some pastry, if you're hungry."

Gomez didn't react.

Matt was tired, annoyed and concerned. That mixture shortened his patience. "Help yourself," he grumbled as he took his coffee and returned to scanning the *Canfield Courier*. Even after two and a half days at the estate, he wasn't accustomed to a newspaper that reported at length on crop and livestock futures and barely mentioned the rest of the world.

"Is she still as upset?"

Matt didn't look up as he answered. "The pills Dr. Howard left make her sleep. When she isn't sleeping, she's pretty broken up."

"They were close, you know."

Matt met the other man's eyes. He got the feeling that Gomez was working his way up to telling him something. The same feeling told him if he pressed the issue, Gomez would retreat into his usual mode— seen but not heard.

"I know."

Gomez made a slurping sound as he took a sip of coffee. Matt guessed that such a breach of etiquette was probably the reason Faircloth held the man in such low esteem.

"I, um..." Gomez paused and lowered his eyes. "Me and DeLancey, well, we have a... I've been looking out for her, too. Ever since that night."

Matt nodded. "What night?"

Gomez shrugged. "I was the one who found her and brung her to Mrs. P."

Scratching the stubble of his unshaven chin, Matt prompted, "Found her?"

Gomez's beard twitched, as if he might be smiling. "She was so scared. Mrs. P. took her in without no questions."

"How old was she?"

"Young. Fifteen or thereabouts."

"Where did you find her?"

"Cemetery at the west edge. We've always figured that her family was buried there. DeLancey never told us for certain, though."

"Didn't anyone call the police?"

Gomez looked genuinely surprised. "Wasn't any call to do that. We asked around. The sheriff said there wasn't no reports of a missing girl. Doc Howard checked her out."

"Why?" Matt asked.

"Just making sure she wasn't hurting."

"Why wasn't she placed in foster care?"

Gomez blinked. "We didn't need no government agencies. She was welcome here."

Matt stared incredulously at the man. "What about finding her family?"

Gomez shrugged. "DeLancey wanted *us* to be her family."

Something about the story didn't gel for Matt.

"The law says you can pick your friends, not your family. And definitely not when you're fifteen."

The small portion of Gomez's face visible above the beard colored red, and anger narrowed his eyes. "It was all legal, like," he said defensively. "I don't want to spend time telling tales out of school. That ain't what I come up here for."

"So what do you want?"

Gomez shuffled his feet. "I came up to ask you to leave."

Matt was tempted to laugh in the guy's face. "I'll leave when DeLancey asks me to."

Gomez shook his head. "Not permanently. I'd just like to sit with her a while. Once them attorneys get done, DeLancey and me, well, we'll be out on our own. 'Sides, if she feels better when she wakes up, I've got a few things I need to say."

"No problem," Matt said, understanding. "I think it would be good for her."

Gomez's anger appeared to turn to embarrassment. "I'm obliged, Mr. Tanner."

Matt was fairly certain Gomez wasn't accustomed to being obliged to anyone. Though he was willing to do as the caretaker asked, he wasn't exactly happy about it. His desire to be there for DeLancey almost convinced him to change his mind. However, he knew his needs shouldn't supersede those of an emotionally distraught woman.

"If I take a ride to Camden, will that give you enough time?"

"Yep. Thanks."

Matt showered, changed and was in his car less than an hour later. His reservations about leaving DeLancey lingered as he tried to focus on the task at hand. The drive into Camden took him a while. When he finally reached the town, he went directly to the hall of records.

The building was as old and graceful as the town. The gentleman assigned to the desk looked as if he might have been there since Day One. He was small and frail and had hearing aids in both ears. Which went a long way toward explaining why Matt had to pound the bell four times before the man looked up from the book in his hand.

He shuffled over to Matt, buttoning his tattered sweater as he moved. "What can I do for you, son?"

Matt retrieved a folded list from his pocket and asked for the records on three cases he had unearthed when he was in Charleston.

The elderly gentleman cocked his head as if he hadn't heard right. "I thought you asked me about records that are ten or more years old. I must not have heard clearly."

Matt smiled. "Yes, that's right—I want all the public records on the Dale Patrick murder in 1985, the Larry Calloway murder in 1981 and the Stafford murders in the late 1970s."

The man whistled as he reached under the counter and pulled out some forms. "I'll need you to fill these out, and then it might take me a couple of hours to get what you need."

Matt nodded. "That's fine. I'll go to the newspaper office and make a few other stops." He glanced at his watch. "You think you'll have these things by, say, two?"

"I know I can get my hands on the stuff. Incidentally, the Stafford murders were in 1976. I should be able to have your copies made by early afternoon."

"Thanks," Matt said, and he filled out the forms and left the required deposit.

By the time he left the building, the sky was filling with threatening clouds. Matt decided to leave his car in the covered lot. After asking directions from a street vendor, he walked the few blocks to the newspaper office.

To his relief, he found an impressive, state-of-the-art newsroom. He hoped their computerization included the archives. In accordance with the directory, he took the elevator to the basement level.

"Hello, sugar," a buxom woman greeted him with a broad smile. "What can we do for you?"

Matt guessed the woman was somewhere in her late forties, although her breast implants were of a more recent vintage. "I'd like to check your archives on these three murder cases."

She frowned as she read his list and tapped each word with a bright pink, one-inch fingernail. "What on earth would you want with this stuff?" She lifted eyes made Elizabeth Taylor-violet by contact lenses.

Waving her hand, she said, "You sure don't look like one of them pervert types."

Her heavy perfume engulfed him in a vapor lock. "I'm doing research for a book."

She brightened instantly. "If I help you, will I be in the book?"

Matt smiled. "Possibly."

She fairly squealed with delight. "Then I'll just go and see what I can find for you. Stay right there, sugar. You hear?"

Matt nodded, waited until she had disappeared into the maze of old file cabinets, then he fanned the scent of her perfume from his face. He glanced around. The woman had tried to make the dingy basement brighter. He smiled when he saw the collection of troll dolls with bright pink hair. There was an assortment of pens and pencils, all with pink pompoms on the ends. Even her government-surplus metal desk was painted pink.

The signature-pink lady returned carrying a small stack of paper. "This is all we have on microfilm," she said. "It's ten cents a page." She moistened one finger and counted the pages.

After thanking the woman, Matt took the still-warm copies.

"Just in case you need anything else, I put my number on the top page."

Matt nodded. As he headed toward the elevator he heard her call, "The second number is my home phone. Call anytime, sugar!"

Matt stopped at a small luncheonette and got a sandwich and a drink to go. With the blazing sun tempered by clouds, he decided to find a shady spot to eat while he read the newspaper articles.

He found himself at the entrance to the Carolina Military Academy. A plaque on one of the columns told him the academy was a private, military-style boarding school founded in the nineteenth century. Matt approached the boy guarding the entrance and inquired if he could walk the grounds.

The young man explained which of the buildings were public and which were private, then handed Matt a commercially produced map of the school. He found a small pond with secluded benches. In the distance he heard the sounds of a band practicing patriotic songs, interrupted every so often by the bark of a commanding voice.

The only other distraction was an egret perched on a rotting log nearby. It was so still, Matt thought it was a statue.

He took his sandwich out of the bag and read as he ate. Every now and then he would take his pen and highlight a phrase. The articles did little more than verify the few details he had already documented. He hoped there would be something in the police reports from the hall of records that could shed some light on the three cases.

Matt had more than an hour to kill, so he decided to explore the school. He put his trash in one of the receptacles that lined the pathway as he walked toward the armory building. He toured that, as well as three other buildings. The architecture was interesting, the history of the school well documented, but he was growing bored.

Until he entered the chapel.

As he listened to the piping voices of young boys practicing hymns at the front of the small, oval church, Matt quietly walked around the room. The walls were adorned with the usual religious symbolism. Interspersed with the those images, Matt found a series of testimonials for everything from generous donations to the school to memorials to fallen alumni.

The last engraving on the far wall caught his attention. It was in memory of Dr. Trevor Walsh, a professor of history at the school for more than a decade. For some reason, the simple memorial gave Matt a chill. Maybe because he couldn't help but wonder if his own life was going to be measured similarly. Unlike his sister, Ellie, and his brother Dylan, Matt was not married. The only contribution he had offered society so far could easily be etched in a stone and forgotten.

"Time to go," he muttered. His rather gloomy and self-indulgent musings were probably the result of spending so much time reading about horrible crimes, as well as his vivid memory of Mrs. Pembleton's lifeless body being removed from the house.

Matt was ready to get back to the living—to DeLancey. He picked up his material from the hall of records and retrieved his car for the trip home. He pressed the speed limit most of the way and was there before four o'clock.

He parked behind a Mercedes, a tan sedan and a sheriff's car in the horseshoe-shaped drive. With a sense of foreboding, Matt left his research materials in the car and started up the steps.

That's when he heard DeLancey scream.

Chapter Six

"Oh, thank God!" DeLancey cried when she saw Matt come through the door. She turned to the men beside her. "This is Matt Tanner. He's been eating my food ever since we got here."

"What's up?"

DeLancey looked at him, hoping the fear she felt wasn't betrayed in her expression. "This is Sheriff Beltram." She pointed a shaky finger at the tall, thin law enforcement officer. "The coroner, Dr. Mangold, and you know Alan already."

DeLancey was pleased when Matt showed his solidarity by not extending a hand to any of the men. "Matt, they've decided that I murdered Mrs. Pembleton."

"Now, DeLancey," the sheriff began, "we aren't accusing you of anything just yet. We're only trying to find out how all that arsenic got into Mrs. Pembleton's body."

"Arsenic?" Matt repeated blankly.

DeLancey nodded. "Apparently someone screwed

up some test results, and they think Mrs. P. was murdered.''

Dr. Mangold stiffened and grasped the lapels of his suit coat with both hands. "I didn't base my findings solely on the hair, urine and fingernail samples. The mortician contacted me when he saw how jaundiced the body was."

"I told you!" DeLancey wailed. "She's been very sick. Isn't jaundice a sign of kidney problems?"

"Yes," the coroner acknowledged. "But when I examined the body, I also found exfoliative dermatitis as well as—"

"Exfoliate what?" DeLancey demanded.

Matt took her hand and said, "A rash that causes the skin to flake. What else?" Matt asked the doctor.

"Advanced skin cancer."

DeLancey let out a breath and glared at Alan. "I told you she had some kind of cancer."

"But the cancer didn't kill her," the doctor said. "The autopsy—"

"You allowed them to carve her into pieces?" DeLancey demanded of the attorney. "Shouldn't you have consulted Dr. Howard before you let them do such an invasive procedure?"

Alan shrugged. "When the sheriff approached me with the suspicions of foul play, I thought an autopsy would prove that his suspicions were unfounded. Will you please calm down? I'll show these men into my parlor. Please join us when you're more composed."

"*His* parlor?" DeLancey muttered when the men

had left the foyer. "We haven't even given Mrs. P. a proper burial and he's already moving in."

She squeezed Matt's hand without thinking. Meeting his concerned eyes, she asked, "Do you really think someone would murder a helpless old woman?"

"Given enough motive."

"Alan," DeLancey decided. "He gets everything. If Mrs. P. really was murdered, Alan is the only possible suspect."

Matt gave her hand a gentle tug. "Let's go hear them out."

DeLancey walked into the parlor, where she and Matt sat down on the settee. She gave the coroner and the sheriff a passing glance, then scowled at Alan with the whole of her being. If he noticed, he gave no sign.

The sheriff reached into his pocket and took out a small pad and a pen. He licked the tip of the pen, then turned his attention to her. "Now, Miss Jones, Mr. Faircloth has informed us that you prepared all of the deceased's meals?"

"Aren't you going to read her her rights?" Matt asked.

The sheriff seemed flustered. "This isn't an official interrogation, it's an interview."

"An interview you've started by asking Miss Jones to offer potentially incriminating information."

"Are you her attorney?"

Matt shook his head. "I'm just a friend."

"Perhaps we should continue this in private," Alan suggested.

"He stays," DeLancey said. She turned and thanked him with her eyes. "It's okay, Matt. I don't have anything to hide. Yes, Sheriff Beltram, I came up every other week on average. Yes, I brought food with me for Mrs. Pembleton and for Mr. Gomez."

"Joe Gomez?" the sheriff asked, turning to Faircloth for confirmation.

"Cousin Esther kept him around out of a sense of duty. He doesn't do much besides creep around."

"Alan, that isn't true, and you know it. Gomez works as a caretaker here," DeLancey explained. "He takes—took care of the house and Mrs. Pembleton."

Alan waved his arm. "Judging by the condition of the estate and my cousin's untimely demise, Gomez wasn't doing a very good job of taking care of anything."

DeLancey felt her cheeks warm. "Maybe that's because he was too busy doing the things you couldn't be bothered to do."

Alan seemed unmoved by her implied accusation. "Please forgo the hysterics, DeLancey. This is about *your* part in the poisoning. Your feelings for me are both irrelevant and pointless, since we won't be keeping company much longer."

"Fine with me," she answered "I don't really want anything to do with a backstabbing killer."

"Sheriff," Alan said with a sigh, "perhaps De-Lancey will be a little more rational in a day or two."

"Perhaps DeLancey *is* being rational," Matt said. "As I understand things, you *are* the only heir, Mr. Faircloth."

DeLancey noticed that, though all her attempts to goad the man had failed, Matt's simple, calmly delivered comment apparently had him seeing red.

"This is hardly your concern, Mr. Tanner," he snapped.

"Not the way I see it. My specialty is criminal justice, and I've learned through my studies that greed is a powerful motivation in family murder situations."

Alan got to his feet. "I would appreciate it if you would begin packing your things, DeLancey. I'll be back around seven to read Cousin Esther's will to you and Gomez. If you see him before then, I suggest you advise him to prepare to vacate his makeshift home in the toolshed, as well."

DeLancey stared at him, annoyed that he was going to take his anger out on Gomez. "Something tells me Gomez will be in a hurry to get away from you."

"I'll be in touch," the sheriff said.

"Then I suggest you get in touch with me in Charleston. Mr. Faircloth has the address and telephone number," DeLancey said.

"Are you going to allow her to leave?" Alan scoffed. "What if she disappears? It isn't like she has a stable past."

The sheriff and the coroner exchanged confused looks. Matt rose and said, "Unless you have legal cause or a charge pending, you can't control DeLancey's comings and goings. Gee, Mr. Faircloth, you should know that. Or did you miss that class in law school?"

"I'll no longer tolerate being insulted in my family home. DeLancey, you'll be asked to leave upon my return this evening. Anything remaining in your room after this evening will be shipped to you in Charleston within thirty days...provided you aren't under arrest by then."

"I'M STARTING to feel like a murderer. I'd certainly like to kill him." DeLancey seethed as she stood at the window and watched Alan shake hands with the sheriff and the coroner before heaving his girth behind the wheel of his Mercedes.

"I think the feeling is mutual," Matt remarked.

He came up behind her. Telling herself that the combination of her sadness at losing Mrs. P., the drugs that had made her a virtual zombie and the emotional shock of learning that someone might have murdered her beloved guardian certainly entitled her to some comforting, DeLancey allowed herself the luxury of leaning against his solid chest.

Matt wrapped his arms around her, cradling her in his strength. It felt good to be held. Too good.

"You must be sorry you tagged along, huh?" she asked as she stepped away.

"I'm glad I could be here for you."

Lord, but I wish he would stop saying just the right things at just the right time. She had neither the strength nor the desire to play cat-and-mouse games just now. Gathering strength from her severely depleted reserve, DeLancey turned and met his kind, concerned gaze. "We'll leave tonight. You don't mind driving in the dark, do you?"

"I'm at your disposal. But are you sure you want to cave in to Faircloth?"

She attempted to smile. "I've known this day was coming since I got here at the age of fifteen."

"How *did* you get here?"

DeLancey tried to keep her body from stiffening at his innocent question. "Mrs. Pembleton became my guardian. She took me in because I didn't have any family."

"What happened to them?"

"It's a long story, and I'm tired," she said, hedging. "I'm going to go up and take a shower before I start packing."

"Anything I can do?"

Stop making me want to tell you my secrets! "If you see Gomez around, clue him in on Alan's ultimatum."

"What about the murder?"

"What?"

Matt shrugged, then asked, "What if Gomez had something to do with Mrs. Pembleton's death?"

She shook her head, waved her arms and answered

unequivocally. "There's no way Gomez would have hurt Mrs. Pembleton. He respected her. He devoted his whole life to her."

"Why?"

"They go way back. Gomez worked for Mrs. Pembleton before she married. I think he's the second or third generation of Gomezes to work for the Tillman family."

"No room for doubt?"

DeLancey met his eyes. "None."

"You go do your thing, I'll see if I can find Gomez."

"Thanks," she said as she tentatively reached out to give his forearm a little squeeze. "I'll be ready to leave long before Alan arrives. I should have told him not to bother. Mrs. P. told me years ago that Tillman land should stay in the Tillman family. Besides, I've never expected anything from her. She gave me so much before she…" DeLancey's voice trailed off.

"No problem. I'll be back to give you a hand."

DeLancey climbed the stairs with legs that seemed to be made of lead. Her brain was still slightly fogged by the drugs Dr. Howard had given her. The notion that someone had harmed Mrs. P. was hard to accept. Almost as hard as learning to accept that Mrs. P. was no longer going to be a part of her life.

As she stepped into the shower, DeLancey began to sob quietly as she mourned her friend and mentor. Burying her face in her hands, she stood under the water until there were no more tears left in her body and no more hot water in the pipes.

After drying her hair and pulling on some jeans and a T-shirt, she walked into one of the guest rooms and found a couple of empty boxes. In her room, De-Lancey decided to pack the sentimental items first—pictures, awards, scrapbooks. Certain Alan would waste no time in tossing away any reminders of her, she went down the hall to Mrs. P.'s room.

Someone—Gomez or Matt—had straightened the bed. DeLancey reached for one of the framed items Mrs. P. kept next to her bed like a proud grandmother, but realized something was missing. Actually, two things. A photograph of DeLancey with Mrs. Pembleton and Gomez taken during her first summer at the estate wasn't there. Neither was the envelope Mrs. Pembleton had started to give her on her first day home.

"Weird."

"What?" Matt asked.

She glanced over her shoulder, then returned to her packing. "There's a picture and a letter missing. Did you see them?"

"I saw the outline of the envelope a day ago. Was it something important?"

DeLancey shrugged. "The first night I got here, Mrs. P. was trying to tell me something about a letter. She was too weak and tired to explain at the time, so I left it, thinking we could..."

"What kind of thing would she put in writing?"

Matt asked as he came over and took the heavy box from her hands.

"Probably another check."

"A check?"

"She was always trying to pay me for the food I brought." DeLancey smiled. "She'd insist, and I'd tear it up. It was something of a ritual, but it hasn't happened in a while."

"Why?"

"I guess because Alan started taking care of her checkbook."

Matt raised one brow. "He took control of her money?"

"All I know is what Gomez told me."

"Which was?"

"Mrs. P. stopped paying him directly about a month ago. Apparently Alan sent his little friend Stephen Thomason over to pay Gomez whenever the spirit moved him."

Matt was pensive. "Sounds to me like that gives Faircloth one more reason for hastening Mrs. Pembleton's death."

"Hardly. Mrs. Pembleton used to teach cooking classes here. Whatever money she had couldn't have amounted to much. This house and the land were her only real assets."

"Is that how *you* learned?"

"To cook? Yep." DeLancey led him to her room. It dawned on her as Matt passed over the threshold that this was the first time a man had been in her bedroom, except for Gomez. But then, Gomez certainly didn't inspire the kinds of fantasies Matt Tanner did. It was awkward to move around when the focal point of the room was her bed. "The drugs must have fried my brain," she muttered.

"What's that supposed to mean?"

"Nothing," DeLancey answered, blushing.

"You're blushing, which means you were thinking something you're not proud of."

"Right now I'm not proud of my thoughts. The key word there is *my*."

Matt deposited the box on the bed so quickly that it bounced before settling on the mattress. DeLancey braced herself and hoped she was prepared.

She wasn't.

Matt turned her and pulled her against him, then wrapped his arms around her and pulled her close enough to feel every powerful inch of him. The vast difference in their heights made it easier—DeLancey could bury her face in the folds of his shirt and hide.

"You feel good."

"Let me go." She had intended her statement to sound like a command. Instead it was a high-pitched waste of time. Even *she* didn't believe her own words.

"I don't know what to do."

She had a suggestion, though she knew better than to make it. Besides, Matt sounded genuinely tortured, which in turn made her feel like a creep. The guy had been a complete rock these past few days. He'd stood up for her when Alan and his lackey duo had come to insinuate that she had done something to hurt Mrs. P. She owed him something in return. "You've been great through all this, and I really appreciate it."

She felt Matt stiffen.

"I mean," she said, correcting herself, "I think you were really nice to do everything you've done, considering."

He stiffened even more. "Considering what?"

DeLancey slowly wriggled her palms up so she could place them against his chest. She could feel his heart racing beneath her hands. Complicating matters more, she could hear the pounding rhythm of her heartbeat in her ears. "I was just trying to convey my gratitude."

Matt placed her at arm's length. She looked up to find his expression bland but his gray eyes shimmering. "Consider it conveyed."

"You don't have to get mad," she insisted. "I was thanking you!"

"I'm not asking for your thanks," Matt said.

DeLancey blew an angry breath toward the ceiling as she planted her hands on her hips. "What are you asking for, Matt? I don't have a decoder ring handy to figure out what you expect from me."

He shook his head. "I don't expect anything."

"Then why are you acting like I just kicked your dog?"

"Because I'm not too proud of myself right this instant."

"Excuse me?"

It was his turn to let out a breath of frustration. "Only a real jerk would come on to a woman when she's dealing with as many things as you are. I'm sorry."

DeLancey stepped close enough to reach up and touch his cheek. "Not as sorry as I am."

"What does that mean?"

She smiled. "It means that I find you funny and attractive. I'm impressed by how smart you are. But mostly, I'm scared of you."

Matt slipped one hand behind her back and tugged her closer. "Scared of me? Why?"

DeLancey met his intense gaze and said, "Because you make me feel things I don't want to feel."

"Like what?" he asked, purring.

Her head fell back. "Like now. This! Matt, with everything that's happened, I don't think I could add another complication to my life."

He brushed his lips against her forehead. "What's complicated about this? It seems so simple to me."

"It isn't what I want," she told him. "You aren't the kind of man I want."

His grip slackened. "What kind of man *do* you want?"

"That's just the point," she tried to explain. "He doesn't exist." *Because neither do I.*

Chapter Seven

"They're here," Gomez said as he moved away from the window.

"Who is they?" Matt asked.

"The cousin and his sidekick," Gomez answered, not bothering to hide his contempt. "I'll go and fetch DeLancey."

Matt opened the door, and Faircloth sauntered in with the ferret hot on his heels. At least the ferret had the decency to hang his head. For his part, Faircloth looked things over as if he thought DeLancey and Gomez might have trashed the place in his short absence.

Matt was about to call for DeLancey and Gomez when he heard a series of thuds on the stairs. Leaving the parlor, he found DeLancey and Gomez struggling with an assortment of suitcases and boxes.

"Ever consider making more than one trip?" he teased as he took a large portion of the load.

"Just making sure Alan knows I'm all cleared out."

He helped them stack the items near the front door, with Faircloth and the ferret looking on. With that portion of the festivities over, Matt lingered near the entrance to the parlor while Faircloth took center stage.

He opened his briefcase, then went to stand next to the fireplace, one arm resting on the mantel. He looked as though he was posing for a portrait instead of publishing the last will and testament of Esther Pembleton. He took his time unsealing the envelope and straightening the pages of the document.

He cleared his throat, then began to read the customary legalese. DeLancey looked bored as Faircloth went through the formalities. Faircloth took his time, obviously savoring the role as the new lord and master of Tillman Plantation.

"To Joseph Gomez, I leave the sum of five thousand dollars and a five-acre parcel at the west corner of Tillman Plantation as described in the attached deed."

Faircloth read that portion of the bequest as if it left a bad taste in his mouth. DeLancey reached over and patted the hand of her friend. But if the bequest or the gesture made Gomez happy, his expression certainly didn't betray it. He stared at Faircloth, stony-faced.

"To DeLancey Jones, I leave the sum of ten thousand dollars and any jewelry, paintings, furniture and furnishings in my home at the time of my death."

Matt felt like running to give her a high five. Faircloth puckered as if sucking a lemon.

"To Dr. Benjamin Howard, I leave the sum of five thousand dollars. And finally—" Faircloth paused for effect "—the remainder of my estate, including cash, bonds and real and personal property shall go to Alan Faircloth. In addition, Alan Faircloth is appointed the executor of this document in accordance with state law. Witness my seal this thirtieth day of April, nineteen hundred eighty-six."

DeLancey and Gomez were out of their seats before Faircloth had finished the last syllable. They were moving toward Matt when Stephen Thomason asked them to stay.

Stephen rose, simultaneously taking a document from the inside pocket of his jacket.

"You have something to add, Stephen?" Faircloth asked.

"I'm sorry, Alan," the ferret said with a nervous grin. "I'm terribly sorry and equally embarrassed."

"About what?" A red stain was creeping up Faircloth's thick neck.

Thomason gave his boss a sheepish grin. "I sent you a memo and a copy of this several weeks ago."

"A copy of what?" Faircloth demanded.

"Why, Mrs. Pembleton's new will."

Faircloth looked about five minutes away from a stroke as he walked over and snatched the document from his employee. The red stain engulfed his face as he read through the will. "This is dated a month ago!"

"That's when she asked me to make the changes."

For a minute, Matt thought Faircloth would go for the other man's throat. "This won't stand up in a court of law!" Faircloth thundered. "We all know Cousin Esther could not have been in her right mind if she was in the midst of being poisoned!" Faircloth shoved the document into the ferret's chest.

"I'm sorry, Alan. I assumed that you understood the ramifications of this when I didn't receive any comments back on my memo."

"I never got a memo, just as you'll never get that bogus document entered into probate. Go ahead and read it. Then find yourself another job. Hell, for all I know the three of you conspired in this. She and that filthy hired man poisoned my cousin," Faircloth bellowed as he pointed an accusatory finger at De-Lancey. "Then she gets you to talk the old bird into changing her will. I won't stand for it!"

The ferret looked flustered. "I—I don't know quite what to do."

"Read it," Gomez said.

The ferret had a different version of Mrs. Pembleton's last wishes.

"Mr. Gomez and Dr. Howard are to receive the same specific bequests."

Again, Matt saw DeLancey give her friend's hand a small squeeze.

"Mr. Faircloth is to receive a lump sum of ten thousand dollars," the ferret announced.

DeLancey gasped.

"The remainder of all real and personal property is to go to Miss Jones, and I am to serve as the executor of the estate."

"That's crazy!" Faircloth howled. "I'm the only heir."

"There is an additional clause," the ferret said quickly. "In the event Miss Jones is unable or unwilling to accept the residuary estate, it reverts to Mr. Faircloth."

"You'll be unable," Faircloth snapped to DeLancey. "I'm going to see to it that the sheriff arrests you as soon as possible. I won't let you profit from your crime."

"Blow it out your nose," DeLancey told Faircloth. "It seems to me that as of right now, you're trespassing."

Faircloth stormed from the house, leaving a rather stunned group in his wake.

"I'm sure he didn't mean those terrible things he said about the sheriff," Stephen said. "He'll calm down as soon as he's had an opportunity to review the will at length."

"Sounds like wishful thinking to me," Matt said. "That man has a mission, and I don't think it's to sit idly by while DeLancey takes what he thinks should be his."

"Mrs. P. didn't think it should," Gomez said. "Mr.

Faircloth might be kin, but he wasn't near as kind to her as DeLancey was. She knew her cousin was just hanging around, waiting on her to die."

"I feel so responsible," Stephen murmured, tidying the pages of the disputed will. "I should have followed up my memo. I know how busy Alan gets. I should have made certain that he reviewed the new will."

"Don't worry about it," DeLancey said. "Gomez, since Alan has left Mr. Thomason stranded, would you mind giving him a ride back to town?"

"Nope."

"Thank you, Miss Jones. I'll be in touch."

"I'll contact you, Mr. Thomason," she said as she shook his hand. "I'm going back to Charleston tonight."

"But, there's no need for that now!" Stephen insisted. "The estate is yours."

"I'll be in touch," DeLancey insisted, all but tugging the man to the door. "Thank you."

She closed the door and leaned against it. Matt could tell she was surprised at the turn of events.

"Alan has probably had a coronary by now," she said.

"He did look a little miffed by the meager ten-grand bequest."

"I didn't know she had that much cash. I had no idea she was even thinking of doing this. I would never have agreed."

"Hold on," Matt said. "You aren't thinking of refusing, are you?"

DeLancey met his eyes and said, "Yes, of course."

"WE WERE ALL SORRY," Rose shouted over the construction. "You look like hell, by the way."

DeLancey could always count on her boss's honesty. "Thanks."

"You look like you haven't had a decent meal in a week. This is supposed to be down time for us all. We're supposed to be regenerating for the grand reopening. Speaking of which, I told Jacques to meet us here at four."

"Jacques?"

"Jacques L'Errant," Rose said with a lousy attempt at a French accent. "He's applying for the sous chef position. All the way from Paris."

DeLancey nodded. "Great, I'm not going anywhere. Joanna said she'd meet me here on her way home from court."

Rose's green eyes softened. "Are the police in Canfield still hassling you?"

"A little. I want Joanna to find some way for me to give Gomez the estate."

"I know you're upset. Hell, who wouldn't be, what with that nasty Alan Faircloth planning the funeral without even consulting you. I know you were close to her, but you have to be sensible. She apparently wanted you to have the estate."

"I'm doing what's right," DeLancey insisted. Stephen had sent her forms to transfer the property and get title insurance, as well as a variety of releases. The forms asked for family information. What on earth was she supposed to do about that?

"Giving to charity is right," Rose said, scoffing. "Giving up a country estate full of antiques and a bank account with six figures is *stupid.*"

A smartly dressed man entered the restaurant, saving DeLancey from having to explain her motives to Rose. Not that she ever could explain.

"I am Jacques L'Errant. You must be Miss Jones," he said as he extended his hand to Rose.

"I'm Rose Porter, the owner. That's DeLancey over there," she said as she pointed to where De-Lancey was perched on a bar stool sipping a soda.

"This *child* is your chef?" he asked in thickly accented English.

The man didn't need good verbal skills to convey his disgust. His pointy face scrunched up as he gave her a once-over.

"Think of me as your child boss," DeLancey said as she stood. "And I'll think of you as my aging assistant."

Jacques looked at Rose. "You did not tell me I would be working for a child."

Rose stood toe-to-toe with the man and said, "You want the job or not?"

"I have trained under master chefs on two continents," Jacques proclaimed.

"We need a sous chef with pastry skills," De-

Lancey said. "Did any of the master chefs you worked with teach you those?"

"Of course," he sputtered.

"Then I don't see the problem. Either you want the job or you don't," Rose said. "I've got a lot of staffing to do before the renovations are completed. I don't have time to waste on attitude, Jack."

"Jacques!"

"Whatever," Rose muttered. "Door number one is the kitchen door. You just came through door number two. You can go through either one—I don't much care."

Apparently Jacques's desire to be in the kitchen won out. He marched past DeLancey into the kitchen with his nose pointed toward the heavens.

"He's a charmer," DeLancey commented. "Should be great to work with."

"I'll keep interviewing."

"If he's good, I don't care about his personality," DeLancey insisted. "Let's give him a chance, at least."

Rose frowned. "I don't get it."

"Get what?" DeLancey returned to her seat and toyed with the straw in her glass.

"You won't give Matt a chance to be nice to you, but you'll give a total stranger the benefit of the doubt."

"Let's not rehash that," she begged of her boss. "I told you, Matt and I aren't compatible."

"You and Jack the French chef aren't compatible,"

Rose argued. "You and Matt are perfect for one another."

"Hardly."

"He's being courted, you know."

DeLancey's head whipped up so fast she probably pulled something. "By who? When did this start?"

Rose patted her heavily teased and bleached hair and pretended to be bored with the whole topic. "I thought you didn't care."

"I don't. I'm just curious."

"Then you shouldn't care that he's captured the attention of one of the most highly regarded women in Charleston."

"I don't. Who is she?"

"She's got connections back to the eighteenth century. She's beautiful, and hordes of men and a few women find her to be the most breathtaking thing in Charleston."

"Men *and* women?" DeLancey repeated. "Matt didn't impress me as the type who liked that sort of adventurous life-style."

"Maybe he just got tired of you rejecting him at every turn."

"You do need help," Joanna Langston announced as she walked into the dining room. "If Rose has selected your ideal man, it's easiest just to accept it. Go with the flow. That's what I did."

Rose greeted her daughter-in-law with a kiss on the cheek. "As I recall, you had the nerve to resist my son in the beginning."

"A momentary lapse," Joanna joked. "Or maybe it was because Gabe was a domineering son of a gun before I whipped him into shape."

DeLancey laughed. She knew there was absolutely no truth to Joanna's claims. She'd seen the couple and their beautiful daughter, Anna Rose. They were a perfect, ideally suited couple who exuded enough love to border on the saccharine.

"So who is DeLancey's soul mate?"

"Matt Tanner."

"Dylan's brother?" Joanna asked as she slipped behind the bar to pour herself a glass of water. "He's definitely handsome. Nice family, if Dylan is any indication." Joanna gave Rose a bright smile and added, "Plus you'd have a mother-in-law in New York, so..."

"You'd have to pay a baby-sitter," Rose teased. "How is my little princess?"

"Spoiled and beautiful, just like her father," Joanna answered. When she spoke of her family her whole face changed. The razor-sharp wit and the biting humor vanished. There was nothing in her green eyes but great pride and an even greater love. "What's up, DeLancey? Besides the fact that you're fighting a losing battle. If my mother-in-law decrees it, then Matt is the man for you."

"Thanks. Kendall said the same thing when she came by yesterday."

"How are Cousin Kendall and her slightly strange husband?"

"Be nice," Rose warned. "My niece loves him. They're building a beautiful family. So what if Jonas sounds like an actor in a bad Civil War epic? They're happy."

"Every time he calls me madam, I feel like I'm running a brothel instead of a law firm," Joanna answered. "I like him. I just think he's a little strange."

"Strange but nice," Rose agreed. "I thought my poor niece would be an old maid before she met him."

"Kendall's in her early thirties, Rose. Hardly matronly," DeLancey said.

Rose gave her pointed stare. "You remind me of her. Kendall thought she was happy devoting her whole life to her career."

"I have a life." DeLancey defended herself.

"I guess that's why you've been here every day since you got back. Or is it that you just like the smell of sawdust?"

"Neither. I thought I was here to help you interview."

"I think I'll go give our sous chef some attitude adjustment. Whatever he's making sure smells good. I'd hate to pass on him just because he's a jerk."

"Do I want to know who the jerk is?" Joanna asked.

"A snooty French chef who didn't like the idea that he'd be working for me. He said I looked like a child."

Joanna smiled kindly. "You could pass for a schoolgirl. Especially dressed like that."

DeLancey glanced at her worn denim shorts and baggy T-shirt. She had long ago kicked off her sandals, so she supposed there might be some merit in the observation. Still, it wasn't very flattering. "I suppose you dress for success when you aren't working?"

"Touché," Joanna conceded. "But I'd never have the nerve to go out without paint and bodywork."

"I'm not very good at putting on makeup."

"And thankfully, it doesn't matter. You look like one of those fresh-faced girls on the soap ads. If I had your skin and eyes, you couldn't get me near a makeup counter."

DeLancey smiled her acknowledgment of the compliment, then changed the subject. "Joanna, I've got a problem. Two, actually."

Joanna nodded as she opened her briefcase. As the clock above the bar moved to four-thirty, Joanna's pocket organizer chirped. "Sorry, old habits die hard," she said as she erased the message flashing— Meet DeLancey—and shut the thing down.

"No problem."

"I know the sheriff in Canfield has asked you to come up for questioning."

DeLancey looked at her quizzically.

"Rose told Gabe and Gabe told me."

"Why didn't I just take an ad out?"

Joanna patted her hand. "She's worried about you,

DeLancey. All that Lycra and lacquered hair is just camouflage for a soft heart. Rose is a wonderful person and she only wants to help you.''

"She can start by keeping her mouth shut. I really don't want the whole town to know I'm a suspect in a murder.''

DeLancey told Joanna the story of Mrs. Pembleton's death and the resulting autopsy. It had been proven that the elderly woman had been poisoned over a long period of time.

"All the tests they did on the food I brought up were negative.''

"That's good," Joanna said as she continued to write furiously.

"They found arsenic in the sugar bowl.''

"Is that a problem?''

DeLancey sighed. "They want me to give my fingerprints. They could be on the sugar bowl. Whenever I was at home, I always took her tray up to her.''

"With the sugar bowl on it?" Joanna asked.

"She had a sweet tooth.''

"Then we'll stall them on the fingerprints. They can ask, but they can't demand until they arrest you or bring you in under official capacity.''

"But won't that make me look guilty?''

"To some people," Joanna admitted. "But it's better to give the authorities as little as possible before they show their hand. Anything else that might cast you in a bad light?''

DeLancey explained about the will. "That's the other part of the problem."

"I'd say so. It does provide you with motive."

"I want you to contact Mr. Thomason for a copy of the will. And I want you to find some way for me to transfer everything to Gomez. I don't want it."

"That's heroic," Joanna said, "but I don't think anyone will buy it. They'll probably assume that you're simply allowing Mr. Gomez to hold the property in trust until the murder investigation fizzles out."

DeLancey shook her head. "You don't understand. I don't want to set up a trust. I want Gomez to have everything. No strings."

"The trust idea was heroic, but giving away an estate with potential value in the millions is lunacy. Unless…"

"I didn't kill her," DeLancey said softly.

Matt came in the front door, looking like a man on a mission. His dark hair was mussed, as if he had been raking his fingers through it. His designer sports shirt looked as if he'd hurriedly pulled it on.

"Have you talked to Gomez?" he demanded of DeLancey.

"Hello to you, too."

"He hasn't called me for two days," Matt said.

"Gomez calls you?" DeLancey asked. "*My* Gomez?"

"Yes. He's been keeping me up to date on the

investigation. I haven't been able to reach him, and I was hoping he had called you.''

With a knot in her stomach, DeLancey reached over the bar, grabbed the phone and dialed Gomez's number.

"No answer," she said. "Maybe he's in one of the fields.''

"Maybe. I'm going up there.''

"Not without me," DeLancey insisted.

"That's not a great idea," Joanna cautioned. "You could be walking right into some sort of sting set up by the sheriff. I strongly advise against going.''

"And I strongly appreciate your advice," De-Lancey said as she gave Joanna a hug. "Tell Rose I'm on my way to Canfield with Matt and I'll call her from there. If I see Thomason, I'll have him get in touch with you. If not, I'll get his number and you can haggle about the will.''

Matt held the car door until DeLancey was safely inside. He bolted around and leaped behind the wheel. In no time, they were on their way to Canfield.

"Did your lady friend mind you abandoning her?''

Matt gave her a quick glance. "What lady friend?''

"Rose told me about her.''

"Rose is confused. I haven't done anything but eat, sleep, work and let you destroy my ego in weeks.''

"What about the person courting you? She said she was beautiful and had some kind of eighteenth-century connections. Rose isn't a liar, Matt.''

He found himself laughing and developing a new

respect for Mrs. Porter. "Rose told you about that, eh?"

"Not that I care. I was only making conversation."

"Okay," he said, cheering up as he watched her cross her arms. She was giving off jealousy signals that went a long way toward improving his mood.

"Why have you been following the investigation?"

"Unsolved crime is my professional field of study."

"I guess that means your personal field of study is co-ed in every sense of the word," DeLancey commented.

This was great! "I don't get your meaning."

"Not that I'm passing judgment. How you float your boat is your business. I just wouldn't have pegged you as the threesome type."

"What on earth did Rose tell you?"

"I wasn't really listening, but I thought I heard her say something about your lady friend being into men and women."

Matt nodded. "I guess it would be correct to say that she's appealing to both men and women."

"I don't think I want to hear anymore."

"She's the kind of lady that draws you back over and over again."

"Thanks for sharing. Now stop."

He signed heavily. "Her lines and curves are incredible."

"How nice for you."

"She's always open and welcoming."

"Wonderful."

"I learn something new every time I'm around her. It's amazing how much I didn't know before—"

"I'm sure I don't want to hear this. Once we find Gomez, the two of you can kick back with some beer and talk dirty."

"I don't think Gomez will be interested. Colleges aren't his thing."

"Colleges?"

"Of course. The lady who has been courting me is Sumter College in Charleston. They want—ouch!" Matt rubbed his shoulder where she had delivered a perfect knuckle punch. "There really isn't a need for violence."

"Appeals to men and women. Learning something new when I'm with her," DeLancey said in a pretty decent imitation of his voice. "You're a moron, Professor."

"I wasn't the one blinded by a jealous rage."

"Jealous rage? That implies some level of interest in you. I don't care what you do, who you do it to or how you do it!"

"Wanna bet?"

"You'll lose," she cautioned.

Matt didn't think so. In fact, he felt so sure he was finally winning that he pulled the car off the road and barely set the emergency brake before reaching for her.

"You said you didn't care who I did it to. Well, I choose you."

"I'd rather remove my own spleen with an oyster fork."

"Then I guess you lose," he said. "Let this be a lesson for you. Never make bets in haste, DeLancey."

"I wasn't talking about myself," she insisted.

"Prove it."

"You are *so* childish," she grumbled, releasing her seat belt.

When she looked at him, he saw a spark of determination in her eyes that looked very much like a challenge. He *never* shied away from a challenge.

"So kiss me and get it over with."

"Why should I?" he asked. "You already lost."

"You're splitting hairs."

"No, I'm thinking it should be you who kisses me."

"I'm thinking it should be me drop-kicking you," DeLancey mimicked. "Come here so we can get this over with."

"I think it would be easier if you came to me. The car isn't that big, and it will be less difficult for you to slip past the gearshift."

"Fine."

The instant he felt her mouth on his, the game was over. This was reality—delicious reality. He had dreamed of this, but the reality was much, much sweeter.

The only way he could keep from grabbing her and dragging her small body into his lap was to remember that this was just a first step. Too much pressure and

she was bound to reject him. That much he had
learned.

Now he was learning that her lips were warm,
moist and incredibly inviting. His knowledge grew as
he felt the outline of her taut breasts pressed against
his arm. When her tongue tested the seam of his
mouth, Matt wondered how long he could keep himself in check.

DeLancey's tiny hands brushed his chest, then the
bare skin on his arm. No matter how soft or tentative
her touch, it left a heated impression on his body. A
body that was quickly filling with passionate arousal.

Matt shoved his hands into the seat leather, afraid
that if he responded, he wouldn't be able to stop. But
respond he did. He couldn't help it. Especially when
she began to slowly press closer to him.

Though he promised himself he would go slow,
easy, it didn't quite turn out that way. He laced his
hands in her silky hair, tilting her head to one side as
he took his first taste of her mouth. It was sheer
heaven. It was perfect.

It had to end.

When it did, DeLancey's passion-laden eyes were
fuel for his ego. At least he knew for certain she
wasn't as immune as she'd had him thinking. He set
her in the seat, praying his pulse would return to normal. He could still smell her perfume on his shirt, still
feel the heat of her lips on his.

"Thank you," he said.

DeLancey colored slightly. "I think I should be thanking you."

Matt smiled. *No recriminations, no regrets. Good, there was nothing to spoil the perfect kiss we shared.*

DeLancey was quiet during the rest of the trip, but Matt didn't mind. He didn't mind anything since DeLancey had silently moved her hand so her fingertips brushed his.

Matt was almost disappointed when the estate came into view. Still, he wasn't callous enough to put his desires above his concern about Gomez.

He parked in front of the main house and followed DeLancey in. The shades were all drawn, and the house smelled close, as if no fresh air had gotten in for a few days.

"Gomez?" DeLancey called as she moved through the house. Their search yielded nothing. The caretaker wasn't anywhere to be found in the house, nor was he visible out any of the windows. "That's weird. He must be in the shed."

"He usually doesn't go in until sundown."

"It's almost that now," Matt commented as he looked at the streaks of purple, pink and yellow painting the late-summer sky.

Walking with DeLancey, it seemed natural to drape his arm over her shoulder. He held his breath at first, steeled for her rebuke. None came.

"Gomez!" DeLancey called as she knocked on the shed door.

There was no sound in response, so she repeated her

actions while Matt walked around the converted shed in hopes of finding a window.

He was at the back of the building when he found a small, dirty window about ten feet above ground level. Glancing around, he spotted an old oil drum and rolled it beneath the window. After testing it for strength, Matt climbed up and wiped some of the grime off the window. It took a few seconds for him to begin to sort out the shadowed outlines of things inside. But then it took no time at all for Matt to recognize Gomez. He was inside, hanging from the rafters.

Chapter Eight

DeLancey watched the commotion from her bedroom window. She turned away only once, when she saw the body bag being carried out. The sheriff's deputies with their flashlights looked like a swarm of lightning bugs.

"I brought you some wine."

She turned to find a weary, somewhat dirty Matt standing in the doorway. He held an open bottle of merlot in one hand, two glasses in the other.

"Thanks."

"I can make coffee or hot chocolate or—"

"Wine works," she said, forcing a smile to her lips. "In fact, wine may be the only thing working around here."

"Are you feeling a little shut down right now?"

She met his eyes. "How did you know?"

He shrugged. "It's common among cops. If you don't learn how to shut down your emotions, you aren't worth a damn at a crime scene."

DeLancey accepted the glass of wine and took a

long sip. "It seems hard for me to believe that two weeks ago the only problem I had was you."

He gave her a thoughtful smile. "I know it's tough right now, but you will get through it."

"I will," she agreed. "I need to know why Gomez would kill himself. It doesn't make any sense."

She looked up and found Matt's face masked in guilt. "What? Did he say something to you on the phone?"

Matt took a fortifying swallow of wine. "He didn't say anything to me. But he left a note."

She grasped his arm. "Did you see it? What did it say?"

Matt put his glass down, lifted hers from her hand and placed it on the dresser, as well. His fingers gripped her upper arms as he softly said, "Gomez admitted he killed Mrs. Pembleton."

DeLancey considered that for a minute, then dismissed it. "That isn't possible. Gomez would never have hurt Mrs. P."

"The note told the cops where to find the rest of the rat poison he'd been sprinkling in her sugar dish for months."

Ripping herself free, she glared at him. "I don't care what the note said. Oh, God!"

"What?" Matt asked as he again held her. "What is it?"

"Gomez must have done this to keep them from suspecting me." She pressed her fingers to her temples. "He knew what an investigation would do to me."

"What would it do?"

DeLancey looked up but couldn't quite wrench the truth from her body. "He knows—knew I'm not up for being accused of a murder I didn't commit."

Matt sat her on the edge of the bed, then closed the door. When he turned around, his face was unreadable. "You have to tell me what's going on, De-Lancey. I can't help you if you aren't honest with me."

"I am honest," she said. "I haven't ever told you anything that I knew was untrue."

"Something tells me you haven't told me everything, either."

DeLancey closed her eyes and tried to imagine what it would be like to tell her secret, confess that she was a murderer and get it all out. "I don't have anything else to tell you," she said, her eyes still shut. "I didn't kill Mrs. Pembleton and I know Gomez didn't, either. I just don't know why else he would say such a thing."

"Neither do I."

She looked into his eyes, and her defenses cracked. "I'm tired and scared, Matt."

"You want to go to sleep?"

"I want something else."

He started to turn, saying, "Some of the pills Dr. Howard—"

"Not that," she said. "I want to lie in your arms. Would you do that for me?"

Matt came to her bedside. She scooted over to make room for him. When he joined her, she quickly curled into the cradle of his body. The slow, even way he stroked her hair allowed her to drift off into a painless sleep.

WHEN SHE OPENED her eyes, it was light out and she was alone. DeLancey ran her fingers over the impression Matt's large body had left on the bed. The blanket was cool, telling her that he had long since abandoned her. It was probably just as well. It wasn't realistic to think he would be around once he discovered the truth.

DeLancey washed her face, brushed her teeth and hair and started down the stairs. She heard voices in the kitchen. Her stomach lurched when she recognized Alan's angry tones. Her gut told her that her life was on the verge of unraveling.

"Good morning," she said as she put on her much-practiced brave front and sauntered over to the coffeepot.

"Well, you must be feeling proud of yourself. Thanks to that softhearted Gomez, you might just get away with murder."

"Go away, Alan. I'm not in the mood for you this morning."

"You might be when the sheriff contacts you."

"Why would the sheriff contact me?" she asked

as she tried to cover the fact that her hands were trembling.

"I had a conversation with him last night."

"I'm sure that made his evening," she said sarcastically.

Alan had a smug smile on his thin lips as he grabbed his car keys off the counter. "Keep it up, DeLancey. Let's see how flippant your responses are when you're hooked up to a polygraph machine. I passed mine yesterday. Now I believe it's your turn."

"Care to tell me why you're shaking?" Matt asked as soon as Faircloth had slithered into his hole.

DeLancey averted her eyes. "Alan is a bully."

"You've never impressed me as the type to be scared of a bully. In fact—" Matt paused long enough to put his arms around her "—I've started to wonder what you're hiding beneath all that bravado."

She rested her head against his chest, gathering strength. "I'm not so full of bravado, Professor. I'm just not like other people."

She felt a soft chuckle rumble in his chest. "I don't believe in aliens, so you can't be all *that* different. Unless you're referring to the fact that you're very beautiful."

"That's only surface."

"True," Matt admitted as he began to stroke her hair. "But I haven't seen anything to tell me you aren't equally lovely on the inside. I can't believe someone as talented and wonderful as you are has self-esteem issues."

You didn't see the blood and the knife in my hand.
"Can you do something other than dissect my personality?"

"Like what?"

"Will you go to the sheriff and get me a copy of Gomez's suicide note?"

"Why?"

"Because I just know I'm right. Gomez wasn't the type to kill himself. He was a fighter."

"I might be able to get a copy of the text."

"Thanks."

"What are you going to do while I'm gone?"

"I've got some stuff to take care of."

"Stuff?" he asked as he held her away and looked down at her face.

"Stuff," she repeated. "Odds and ends."

"Is all this vagueness your way of letting me know it's none of my business?"

Her heart grew heavy when she read the disappointment in his eyes. Still, there was nothing she could do, nothing she could say. "I'm not doing anything illegal or immoral. Isn't that enough for you?"

"If I say no, will you tell me any more?"

She cupped his cheek in her hand. "No."

Matt took her palm and brought it to his lips. After a brief, electric kiss, he said, "Then I guess I'll have to trust you."

"Think of it more as tolerating me," she suggested as she withdrew her hand.

"Call it what you like," Matt said as he grabbed his car keys. "I'll see what I can do about the note."

"Thanks. I'll be here when you get back."

Matt paused and searched her face, then in little more than a whisper, he added. "I'll be here for you no matter what."

As soon as she heard Matt's car leave, DeLancey reached for the phone and called Joanna's office. Unfortunately, her secretary said she was in court. "Please have her call me as soon as possible," DeLancey pleaded. She gave her number in Canfield, and the secretary promised to get it to Joanna during the ten o'clock court recess.

Two hours. DeLancey had to do something. She couldn't bear the thought of sitting in the house for two hours until Joanna could advise her what to do. Besides, she didn't dare sit around in case the sheriff decided to come to take her for a polygraph.

DeLancey decided a walk was a good diversion. Without consciously willing it, she found herself at Gomez's. Her chest tightened when she came upon the scraps of crime-scene tape dangling from the trees around the toolshed. Still, she was drawn inside. Drawn to search for some explanation for her friend's death.

The shed was a wooden shell constructed of planks and boards from some of the old abandoned buildings on the estate. Gomez had taken the remnants and crafted himself a decent, if sparse, living space.

Her eyes went to the rafters. She shuddered when

she saw the fresh gouges in the wood where the noose had been. Swallowing her sorrow and repulsion, she began to look around the room. There were stacks of hunting magazines and a few items of clothing. None of the crudely made furniture had been disturbed. No signs of a struggle. Nothing to suggest the death was anything but what it seemed—a suicide. DeLancey was crestfallen. Gomez had been a big, burly man who surely would have fought if someone had put the noose around his neck. But there was nothing out of place, nothing to support her belief that Gomez had been a victim.

She emerged from the shed and kept walking. The moist grass smelled fresh and clean. The tree leaves rustled on a soft breeze. The summer sun was warm against her skin, and she felt a certain serenity walking aimlessly through field after field of high grass.

DeLancey knew every inch of the farm. She'd spent hours roaming the land during her first years with Mrs. Pembleton. Her mind returned to that time, to all the old emotions. First the fear that Mrs. Pembleton would turn her over to the police. Then the gradual trust, which allowed her to finally admit to the woman what little she remembered about that night in the cemetery when Gomez had found her, wet, shaking and bloody. Even when she had told of the knife she'd hidden behind one of the headstones, Mrs. Pembleton hadn't so much as batted an eye.

DeLancey wondered if it was possible to get lucky twice in a lifetime. Was it possible that Matt would be as understanding? That he would know the monster she had been back then no longer existed?

DeLancey suddenly realized she was standing at the entrance to the cemetery. She wondered what guilt had brought her to this place. She had returned here only once in ten years, shortly after she'd been found, so Gomez could retrieve the hastily hidden knife. Since that day, neither Mrs. Pembleton nor Gomez had ever mentioned it. Now both were dead.

Maybe she wanted to punish herself. Maybe she was just feeling morose. DeLancey dropped on her stomach and slipped beneath the locked gates. Once inside, she looked around. The old tombstones leaned at odd angles, thanks to centuries of rain and shifting soil. The graveyard was haphazardly tended. She wondered who had taken the time to maintain the grass and support some of the crumbling stones.

The mausoleum where she'd taken shelter was ahead, past the graves of those more recently interred in the old cemetery. As she walked, her brain flashed memories of rain, blood and confusion. She also got a flash of something else. Of someplace else.

That place was suddenly so vivid and terrifying that she stood perfectly still and closed her eyes to concentrate. It was a room with yellow paint and floral curtains. Then the floral curtains were splattered with blood.

Shivering, she opened her eyes and hugged her arms to her chest. Was the house with the yellow room and the floral curtains the place where she had killed someone so long ago?

The only other snippet of memory she had retrieved in all these years had something to do with a creek or a stream. She remembered torrents of rain and swirling current. She remembered being afraid and feeling an almost overwhelming need to escape. She'd reasoned that it was probably a memory of how she had left her crime scene. Thinking she might be able to find the place, she had walked every inch of the creek that bordered the back of the estate. But nothing ever seemed familiar. The fragment of memory had yielded little over the years except a fear of water.

"I'm tired of being afraid," she whispered. "I'm tired of hiding. I'm tired of not knowing." She thought of Mrs. Pembleton and of Gomez. She smiled when she remembered how Gomez had led her from the cemetery that night, using his odd mixture of kindness and gruffness.

DeLancey reached the steps of the mausoleum. She saw a dark spot on the marble step, bent to touch it, then let out a gasp. The tips of her first two fingers were red with...blood. She saw a second drop, then a third. She followed the trail, struggling to keep the past and the present separate. It wasn't easy. The blood trail led her into the cool stillness of the building. Her breath caught in her throat when she reached the crypt of DeLancey Jones—the real one, the one from whom she'd taken her name. Then she screamed.

With her cry echoing off the walls, DeLancey used her trembling hand to wipe the smear of blood off the commemorative stone. At the base of the stone she found two things.

The first was a knife identical to the one she had discovered in the pocket of her dress all those years ago. Taped below the knife was a color photocopy of the photograph that had gone missing from Mrs. Pembleton's bedside table.

"Someone knows," DeLancey whispered, terrified. She wiped her hands on her shorts and ran from the building.

She was vaguely aware that she had cut her arm on the rusty fence as she shimmied under it. Her thought was to get to the only home she'd known. Though her chest burned, she didn't stop running until she reached the house.

She entered through the back, closed the door and tried to get her violently shaking hands to lock the rarely used security chain into place.

"No luck on the note. Good Lord! What happened to you?"

DeLancey jumped and let out a cry as she whirled to find Matt in the kitchen. She couldn't speak, still shaking with terror. Abandoning the grocery items he had gotten on his way from the sheriff's office, he came around the counter.

"Is there a reason you're covered in dirt and paint?"

"Paint?"

Matt came close enough to get a better look at the red stains on her shorts, hands and arms. "All except that," he concluded, pointing to the jagged scrape on her upper arm. "My guess would be a rusty nail. What were you doing?"

"Walking," she said. "This isn't blood?"

He had taken one of the linen napkins from the sideboard and used it to apply pressure to her arm. "Blood? Did someone do this to you? Is that why you're shaking?"

He was glad he was holding her arm, since her knees buckled at that moment. Matt took her to a chair and made sure she was stable before kneeling in front of her. "What is going on, DeLancey?" he asked, taking her quivering hands in his.

Her brown eyes shimmered before silent tears spilled down her cheeks. "I just got spooked."

"Where did the dirt and the paint come from?"

"Paint?" she repeated softly. "It's paint? You're sure?"

"Except for your arm, which needs a thorough cleaning and a bandage. What did you cut it on?"

"The gate," she answered in a strangely calm tone.

"When was your last tetanus shot?"

''Tetanus shot?''

Matt placed his finger beneath her chin. Lifting her face, he wiped away the damp, dirty tear tracks and looked into her terror-filled eyes. ''I'm going to call Dr. Howard. I think you might need some more of his nerve-numbing pills. I'll ask him about the cut.''

As he went for the phone, Matt could hear her mumbling about paint, about being cold. She seemed slightly hysterical. Maybe the sudden and violent deaths of the two people she was closest to had broken her.

A few minutes later, Matt had the doctor on the line. He explained what little he knew, then asked for advice.

''Sounds like an anxiety episode. Make her take two of the pills I left. Keep pressure on her arm until the bleeding stops. I'll be there shortly.''

''Thanks.''

''Did she say anything else? Anything at all?'' the doctor asked.

''She isn't making a lot of sense right now,'' Matt answered.

''Do you know where she was?''

''She's covered in dirt and paint, so my guess would be she might have gone to the toolshed.''

''That could explain it. Going to the site where her friend committed suicide is certainly enough to bring on a severe situational anxiety attack.''

For a country doctor, Howard was obviously well

versed in psychological matters. "Thanks. I'll be waiting for you."

Matt went to the cabinet and found the pills Dr. Howard had left. As he was breaking off one of the tamperproof squares, he realized two of the pills had been removed from their plastic packaging.

Returning to DeLancey, he found her only slightly less upset. "When did you take these?" he asked, holding the empty packaging in front of her.

"Take what?"

"The pills. There's two missing. I can tell. Whenever I've given them to you, I've tossed the wrapper, as well."

DeLancey blinked twice. "I haven't taken any."

"Are you sure?" Matt pressed. "I have a feeling these little bombs are intended to be taken as prescribed."

"I haven't taken any, and I don't want to take any now."

"You aren't dealing with choices," Matt said. "Take these, and then we'll go upstairs and get you cleaned up before the doctor gets here."

After taking the pills, DeLancey smiled, then began an eerie laugh. "It's only paint," she repeated. "Only paint."

"Let's get some of this crud off you."

"I can wash without help, thanks."

He thought about arguing with her, but it seemed

pointless. Even in the midst of emotional turmoil, DeLancey's stubborn streak was still intact.

"If you—"

Matt was cut off by the ringing of the phone. He went to answer it and suddenly found DeLancey ducking beneath his arm to grab it off the hook.

"HELLO?"

"It's Joanna."

DeLancey felt a surge of relief. The terror was beginning to drain from her body, replaced by the fuzziness from the pills she'd ingested.

"Hi."

"I'm in the middle of a court recess, but my secretary said you sounded upset."

"Alan is pressuring the sheriff to get me to take a polygraph."

There was a brief hesitation. "I take it that's a problem?"

Aware that Matt was just a few inches away, she simply answered, "Definitely."

"Look, I'll call the sheriff's office and tell him I'm your attorney and that any requests should come to me. That will buy you some time."

"Thanks."

"Don't thank me yet, DeLancey. I'll do this but I can't keep running interference for you until we have a long talk."

"I understand."

"I hope so. Call my secretary for an appointment as soon as possible," Joanna said emphatically. Then, in a softer, less authoritarian tone she added, "As your attorney, anything you tell me is privileged."

"That means you couldn't repeat it, right?"

"Right. So you make an appointment, and I'll make sure Sheriff Beltram understands the concept of due process."

"Thanks."

"I'm glad you're going to confide in Joanna," Matt said as she replaced the receiver.

"I'm considering it."

"Considering?" Matt repeated with annoyance. "DeLancey, you've got to trust someone. You can't keep going like this. You're a mess."

DeLancey looked away. "It isn't as easy as you make it sound."

"It is if you didn't kill Mrs. Pembleton."

"I didn't!"

Shaking his head, Matt replied, "Then you're doing one hell of an impression of guilty."

"Can't you just trust me on this?" she pleaded, afraid of losing his support. "I'm doing my best to clear things up. I just have to do it on my terms."

"What terms are those?"

DeLancey was trying to formulate an answer when the phone rang again. Assuming it was Joanna with news that she had managed to placate the sheriff, at least for now, she grabbed the receiver.

"Hello?"

"Was it like you remembered?" a scratchy male voice asked.

"Who is this?" DeLancey demanded.

Whether it was the panic in her voice or the fear in her eyes, the effect was the same. Matt grabbed the receiver from her and listened for a second or two. Then he turned accusatory eyes on DeLancey.

Chapter Nine

"How is she?" Dr. Howard asked as he entered the house with his medical bag in one hand and a wrapped manila envelope under his arm.

Matt shrugged. "She's in the tub." Seeing the doctor's concern, he added, "She's not getting her arm wet until you have a chance to check it out."

Inviting the doctor into the kitchen, Matt offered him a drink. Dr. Howard asked for water, explaining that he had a full afternoon of work ahead of him. "Did you find out what upset her?"

Matt shrugged as the feeling of helplessness was renewed. "The first time or the second time?"

"She had a second delusional episode?"

"I wouldn't call it delusional, exactly."

"Are you a psychiatrist, Mr. Tanner?"

"No," he admitted. "But then, neither are you."

"But I was," Dr. Howard corrected him with an air of authority. "I still see a few patients from the old days."

"Sorry. I didn't mean to insult you. I didn't realize you had a specialty."

Howard smiled, apparently hoping to put Matt at ease. "I'm at the twilight of my career, Mr. Tanner. I can assure you it has been both diverse and generally successful. Now, shall we discuss the specifics regarding DeLancey?"

Matt raked his hands through his hair in frustration. "All I know for sure is that she went for a walk. Something or someone threw red paint on her or she fell into it when she was hauling ass, er, butt back here."

Howard gave him a gentlemanly smile. "I am familiar with human anatomy. Please don't feel the need to temper your comments in my presence."

"She came through the door and locked it as if someone was right on her heels."

"Did you see anyone?"

"I looked out, but I didn't see a soul."

The doctor nodded as he absorbed the information. "Did she give you any more specific information?"

"She hasn't given me much but evasion," Matt answered. "However, she did get some phone calls— one from her lawyer."

"DeLancey has her own attorney?" Howard seemed mildly surprised.

"She's working on it. But that wasn't what upset her."

"We don't know that," Howard cautioned. "We

can't possibly know that speaking with an attorney didn't cause her additional stress.''

Matt struggled to keep from rolling his eyes or shaking the man. ''I may not have an M.D., but I'm pretty sure the second call was the one that upset her.''

''Second call?''

''Right after the first,'' Matt explained. ''It was a male voice, muffled, but he certainly made his point.''

''Which was?''

''All I heard was something about 'making like it was.' But I have no idea what 'it' referred to.''

Dr. Howard's only reaction was a slight slip in his paternal expression. ''Did you recognize the voice?''

''Sure. It sounded like hundreds of crank calls I've listened to over my lifetime.''

''There really is no need for sarcasm, Mr. Tanner. You and I have the same goal. I want to help De-Lancey. I have always tried to help her.''

''Always? Does she have a history of going to pieces?'' Matt asked.

''Far from it,'' Dr. Howard insisted. ''She's just a very complex person. Now, I'll go up and see if she's ready to see me.''

''Thanks,'' Matt said.

''Oh,'' the doctor said, ''I found this on the front porch, some sort of package for you.''

Matt took the package and turned it in his hands. No postmarks, no return address. Just his name in black, block letters.

He opened it, stared in disbelief, then spent the next several hours verifying the contents.

DeLancey AWOKE feeling a little better. Rubbing her hands over her face, she tried not to think about what had happened at the cemetery. Then she remembered the call. If the anonymous caller knew the truth, it was only a matter of time before the rest of the world knew.

She sat back, pounding her head against the pillow as she fixed her eyes on the last streams of daylight filtering through the curtains. Obviously someone had put it all together. She only wished she could. Maybe, after all, it would be good to be able to remember everything. Maybe she had a reason to do what she had done all those years ago. If she knew that, maybe she could have a decent shot at a normal life.

DeLancey sucked in a breath and tried to formulate a plan. What should she do? A decent person would simply surrender. A decent person would face whatever punishment lay ahead. "But I don't want to be decent," she muttered. "Not until I remember what I did and why."

She could run. It would be simple to disappear, take on a new identity and start over. Mrs. Pembleton had shown her how easy that was long ago, when it was time to register for school. Somehow, her guardian had managed to get her a birth certificate. Once she had that, DeLancey had gotten a driver's license, social security card and a new chance at a life.

But starting over would mean leaving Rose, Shelby and all her friends at the Rose Tattoo. It would mean never seeing Matt Tanner again.

Matt should have been the least of her concerns. But he wasn't. She had managed to keep herself safe by never getting involved. But Matt's pursuit had been both relentless and persuasive. There were times when she allowed herself to imagine what it would be like to let herself fall in love with him. To experience the feeling of being connected to another human being in the most intimate way. To finally let go and surrender to those feelings she'd fought since meeting Matt.

"And he can write to you in jail," DeLancey muttered as she got out of bed. She'd come to at least one decision. Maybe she couldn't live happily ever after. That didn't mean she couldn't spend her last night at Tillman with him. Then she would simply slip away.

Still wondering if she was making the right decision, she took her time washing and styling her hair. After spritzing her body with her favorite perfume, DeLancey mustered courage as she dressed. Seducing Matt shouldn't be a problem, not if the one kiss they had shared was any indication. The hard part would be leaving when it was over.

MATT WAS RELIEVED when DeLancey entered the room looking calm and refreshed. "I was wondering if you'd get up. Hungry?"

Her eyes seemed to darken seductively at his innocent question.

"Are you feeling better?"

She shook her head. "Other than the fact that I've pretty much lost my mind, I'm great."

"Sorry I asked," he said. "I've got some news."

"Can it wait a little bit?"

Something in her tone made him look at her more closely. DeLancey was dressed in a kind of casual chic. Her dress was far more feminine than anything he could recall her wearing. In fact, it was the first time he had ever seen her wearing anything other than a uniform or shorts.

When she rummaged in the refrigerator, Matt was treated to an unobstructed view of her tush. And quite a tush it was, he thought with a wicked little grin. He was still wearing that grin when she turned unexpectedly, catching him in the act. *Man, I'm a pig!*

"Is something wrong, Professor?" Her voice was deep, seductive.

"No." Matt cringed when he heard the crack in his voice. "Nothing," he added in a more even tone.

"You don't seem yourself," she said, and began walking toward him.

He took an involuntary step back when she was close. The action didn't go unnoticed, not if her satisfied smile was any indication.

"DeLancey," he cautioned as he held one hand, palm out. "Whatever has gotten into you, I don't think now is the right time. We shouldn't do this."

"I haven't done anything."

He backed up again, only to find himself against the cool wall. DeLancey kept coming, her intense eyes belying the small smile curving her delicate mouth.

"Please?"

Without a word, Matt took the soda can from her hand and deposited it on the nearest table. He switched their positions and flattened his palms on the wall on either side of her head. "I'm a human being, DeLancey. I don't know what's come over you, but I'm not made of stone. Stop playing around."

SHE COULD SMELL his musky cologne and hear his slightly uneven breath. There was a smoldering intensity in his eyes that sent a ripple of desire into the pit of her stomach.

"Who said I was playing?"

"I have a feeling I won't respect myself in the morning," he whispered.

His warm, mint-scented breath washed over her face. Tilting her head back, she searched his eyes beneath the thick outline of his eyelashes.

"I know this is wrong," he said. Then, bending at the waist, he leaned forward until his lips barely grazed hers. Wide-eyed, DeLancey experienced the first tentative seconds of the kiss through a haze. The pressure from his mouth increased almost instantly. It was no longer tentative or regretful. It was demanding and confident, apparently fueled by all the accidental touches and meaningful looks that had punctuated their tense coexistence during the past few days.

His hands moved slowly, purposefully to her waist. His strong fingers slipped beneath the fabric of her blouse, coming to rest just below her rib cage. Her mouth burned where he incited fires with his expert exploration of her mouth. A sigh inspired by purely animal desire rose in her throat. She was being bombarded with so many sensations at once, each more pleasurable than the last. The calloused pad of his thumb brushed her waist. His kiss was so thorough, so wonderful that her knees were beginning to tremble.

When he pulled away, DeLancey very nearly reached out to keep him close to her. It wasn't necessary. He didn't go far. She listened to the harmony of their labored breathing.

"What are we doing?" he rasped.

"I believe you just kissed me."

"Yes, that much I know. I kissed you. You responded. That's why I'm wondering. You've pushed me away since Day One. Why the sudden change of heart? Why are you playing this game?"

"It's not a game," she said, feeling sad and lonely. Maybe her plan wouldn't work, after all. "So what if we both know this isn't such a great idea? Let's just go ahead."

"That," he said as he lifted his head and met her eyes, "is one of the few honest things I've ever heard you say. And I agree. In spite of the fact that I have something I want to tell you and in spite of the fact that my conscience will bother me for the rest of my days, I can't help it, DeLancey. I've wanted you too long to be honorable when you're acting like this.''

Matt wasn't subtle with his second kiss. And there was nothing even remotely sweet about it. The kiss was meant to do one thing, convey desire. Even before he pressed his hardness into her belly, DeLancey knew he was aroused as he'd never been before.

''Wait,'' she said, a little frightened by the level and suddenness of his passion. She placed her hands flat against his chest and gave a little shove. ''Maybe we're moving a little too fast. Maybe this *is* wrong.''

''How can you say that?'' he countered.

She watched him from behind the safety of her lashes. ''I don't do this sort of thing. I don't sleep around for the hell of it.''

''DeLancey.'' He said her name on a rush of breath and confusion. ''I don't want to make love to you for the hell of it. And I'll stop right now, if that's what you want.''

''I thought I knew what I wanted,'' she said.

He looked at her with eyes so full of tenderness she almost sighed. ''I want to make love.'' He brushed his lips across her forehead. ''I find you an incredible mixture of strength and vulnerability. I've never been this off balance with a woman, and it has nothing to do with the recent events in your life. I've felt this way since I first saw you at the restaurant.''

"I guess we don't really need a reason. We *are* adults."

"Tell yourself whatever you want, DeLancey," he insisted as his fingers moved to grip her upper arms. "You're a complex woman, but that's part of your charm. I also know you have feelings for me." His lips touched hers. His voice deepened to a husky whisper as he continued. "We've shared more than meals, DeLancey. Like it or not, there's more here than just lust. I've even grown to like the way you keep putting me in my place."

He kissed her lightly.

"I love the way you laugh. I love the fire in your eyes when you're angry. I love the way you've rejected me over and over."

"Matt?" she whispered, feeling her plan crumble. After words like that she knew she shouldn't take advantage of his feelings. She started to push out of his embrace.

"Don't fight me, DeLancey, please. I know how good it could be between us, and because of that I don't think I can go on pretending I'm happy with the occasional crumb you toss at me."

"They aren't crumbs," she insisted. "I know you need more, but I—"

He silenced her by kissing her with equal measures of passion and pleading. "I'll give you everything, DeLancey. Trust me."

"This wasn't what I planned," she admitted. "You're confusing me."

"I'm trying not to," he said quietly. His hand came up, and he captured a lock of her hair between his thumb and forefinger. He silently studied the dark strands, his expression intense.

"I don't know what to do, Matt. I don't want to make a mistake. I don't want to hurt you."

"You won't. You can't," he promised, his voice low, seductive.

The sincerity in his voice worked like a vise on her throat. The lump of emotion threatened to strangle her as the silence dragged on.

"We don't have anything in common. We want different things."

"How do you know that? We've never talked about what we want," he countered, his voice as smooth as velvet. "We can do that, DeLancey, and we should, since I have some good news for you. But we'll do it later," he said, scooping her off the floor, cradling her against his solid chest.

Matt carried her upstairs to her bedroom. As if she were some fragile—and infinitely precious—object, he placed her on the bed, gently arranging her against the pillows.

DeLancey remained silent as she watched him shrug out of his shirt before joining her on the bed. Through passion-dilated eyes, she took in the impressive sight of him. Rolling on his side, Matt pulled her closer until she encountered the solid outline of his body. His expression was fixed, his mouth little more than a taut line.

"I'll make it good, DeLancey. So good for you. You'll see," he said, gently pulling her into the circle of his arms.

It felt so good, so right. She needed his strength if she was going to make it through this without losing her mind. Closing her eyes, DeLancey reminded herself that thanks to Matt, she would know what it was like to connect to another person, at least for one night.

She surrendered to the promise she felt in his touch.

Cradling her in one arm, Matt used his free hand to stroke the hair from her face. She greedily drank in the scent of his cologne as she cautiously allowed her fingers to rest against his thigh. His skin was warm and smooth, a startling contrast to the very defined muscle she could feel beneath her hand. She remained perfectly still, comforted by his scent, his touch and his nearness. It all seemed to warm her as nothing else could. Being here in this room with Matt was enough to erase the fear and uncertainty that had plagued her for years. What could be the harm in the few hours of the pleasure she knew she could find here?

"DeLancey?" he asked on a strained breath. He captured her face in his hands, and his thumbs teased her cheekbones. His blue-gray eyes met and held hers. His jaw was set, his expression serious. "I don't know if I have the strength to let you get up and walk away from me now. Please tell me this is what you want. Please?"

He tilted her head back. His face was mere fractions of an inch from hers. She could feel the ragged expulsion of his breath. Instinctively, her palms flattened against his chest. The thick mat of dark hair served as a cushion for her touch. Still, beneath the softness, she could easily feel the hard outline of muscle.

"I want you so badly," he said in a near whisper.

Her lashes fluttered as his words washed over her. She needed to hear those words, perhaps had wished for them in that secret part of her heart. Matt's lips tentatively brushed hers. So featherlight was the kiss that she wasn't certain it could qualify as such. His movements were careful, measured. His thumbs stroked the hollows of her cheeks.

DeLancey banished all thought from her mind. She wanted this desperately. His hands and his lips made her feel alive. The ache in her chest was changing, evolving. The fear and confusion were being taken over by new emotions. She became acutely aware of every aspect of him. The pressure of his thigh where it touched hers. The sound of his uneven breathing. The magical sensation of his mouth on hers.

When he lifted his head, DeLancey grabbed his broad shoulders. "Don't," she whispered, urging him close to her. "I *do* want this, Matt. I want you."

His resistance was both surprising and short-lived. It was almost totally forgotten when he dipped his head. His lips did more than brush against hers. He moved his hands to her small body and crushed her against him. She could feel the pounding of his heart beneath her hands.

The encounter quickly turned intense and consuming. His tongue moistened her slightly parted lips. The kiss became demanding, and she was a very willing participant. She managed to work her hands across his chest until she felt the outline of his erect nipples beneath her palms. He responded to her action by running his hands all over her back and nibbling her lower lip. It was a purely erotic action, one that inspired great need and desire in DeLancey.

A small moan escaped her lips as she kneaded the muscles of his chest. He continued to work magic with his mouth. DeLancey felt the kiss in the pit of her stomach. What had started as a pleasant warmth had grown into a full-fledged heat emanating from her very core, fueled by the sensation of his fingers snaking up her back, entwining in her hair, tilting her head at a severe angle. Passion flared as he hungrily devoured first her mouth, then the tender flesh at the base of her throat. His mouth was hot, the stubble of his beard slightly abrasive. And she felt it all. She was aware of everything—the outline of his body, the almost arrogant expectation in his kiss. Matt was obviously a skilled and talented lover. DeLancey was a compliant and demanding partner.

This was a wondrous new place for her, special and beautiful. The controlled urgency of his need was a heady thing. It gave DeLancey the sense that she had a certain primal power over this beautiful man.

Matt made quick work of her clothes. He kissed, touched and tasted until DeLancey cried out for their joining. It was no longer an act. It was a need. She needed Matt inside her to feel complete. To feel connected.

Poised above her, his brow glistening with perspiration, Matt looked at her with smoldering, heavy eyes. He waited for her to guide him, then filled her with one long, powerful thrust.

The sights and sounds around her became a blur as the knot in her stomach wound tighter with each passing minute, building fiercely until she felt the spasm of satisfaction begin to rack her body. Matt groaned against her ear as he joined her in release.

As her heart rate returned to normal, her mind was anything but. She lay perfectly still, not sure what to do or say. She'd made love to Matt with total and complete abandon. The experience was wild, primitive…and terrifying. Her eyelids fluttered in the darkness as she began to think of the consequences of her rash behavior.

Guilt swept over her like a blanket as she realized the gravity of the situation. It was over. Now all she could do was wait for him to fall asleep. She started to roll out of the sanctuary of his arms.

"Relax, okay? I'm not going anywhere," Matt said against her ear. "I want you to stay with me."

"I'll always be with you," she answered. *And you with me. In my heart, if not my life.*

"You don't know how happy that makes me,

DeLancey. I've never felt this way about anyone. You probably don't want me to say it, but I—"

"Hush," she said as she placed her finger against his lips. "We'll talk in the morning. Right now I'd just like to lie in your arms."

"How can I argue with that?" he retorted as he kissed her forehead.

An hour and a half later, as Matt slept, DeLancey got into a cab in front of the house. A tear slid down her cheek as she said a silent farewell to the man she now knew she loved. And had to leave.

Chapter Ten

Matt climbed the stairs to the studio apartment and shoved open the door to unit 2A without knocking.

"Matt!" DeLancey cried, dropping a coffee mug. "What are you doing here?"

He stormed over to her, opening and closing his fists as his mother's mantra about never hitting a girl played through his mind. "You," he said as he took her arm and sat her on the sofa, "are going to explain."

"Explain what?" she asked. "Just because we slept together one time doesn't mean I have to bare my soul to you."

Matt raked his hands through his hair, reminding himself that DeLancey had a tendency to fight strength with strength. He called on the interview techniques he had learned at the police academy and put his sense of personal betrayal on the back burner.

"I'm not asking you to bare your soul. I'm simply trying to understand why you sneaked out and came here." He glanced at the boxes and suitcases strewn around the small studio, then added silkily, "Going somewhere?"

She squeezed her eyes shut. In a very soft voice, she said, "Don't make this harder than it already is."

"What? If you had stayed in Canfield, you would have heard the news for yourself. Your little disappearing act was a waste of my time *and* yours."

"What?"

Matt sat beside her. "Yesterday I got an anonymous package. It concerned you."

A gasp spilled from her slightly parted lips. "Then…you know?"

He nodded. "Apparently, whoever sent the documents to me also furnished Sheriff Beltram with a copy. Thomason came to the door at one this morning to let you know that Faircloth was in custody."

Her only response was a blank stare.

"Did you hear what I said? Faircloth has been charged with the murders of Mrs. Pembleton and Gomez."

"Wait!" She stood and paced in front of him, twisting a lock of hair around her finger. "The police have proof that *Alan* killed Mrs. Pembleton?"

Matt nodded and held out his hand. Once she accepted it, he tugged her onto his lap. "Faircloth has been skimming money from Mrs. Pembleton for years."

"Alan?"

Kissing the top of her head, Matt held her tightly, glad he had gotten to her before she left Charleston.

"Most of the money is unaccounted for. I'll bet he's socked it away in some offshore account in an island country with lax banking regulations."

"Alan never needed money," DeLancey said. "It doesn't make sense that he would steal from Mrs. P. and kill her. When did they realize that Gomez's confession and suicide were faked?"

"The note, I guess."

"The one he left?"

"It was typed."

She rested her palm on his shirt above his heart. He didn't know if it was a conscious gesture, but he didn't much care. It felt good.

"How would Gomez type a letter?"

"That's what the police wondered. They ran tests on the note, and both the paper and the ink toner matched the computer and printer from Faircloth's Canfield office."

DeLancey's hand was still. "This makes no sense. Alan isn't my favorite person, but I don't see him as a thief and murderer. You saw him when Stephen read the second will! If he was smart enough to cover his tracks by implicating Gomez, don't you think he would have made sure he was in line to inherit?"

"So it's a little neat," Matt conceded. "But it means you have no reason to run."

He felt her stiffen. "What if the police are wrong? What if their arrest of Alan is premature?"

Matt sighed, touched her face and tilted it toward him. He saw the fear in her eyes and gently kissed her forehead. "If you tell me what has you so scared, maybe I can help. I was a cop for eight years, De-Lancey. I'm good at solving problems."

She scooted off his lap. "You can't help me. No one can," she told him. "I'm leaving Charleston as soon as I can get packed."

"Why? I know you didn't kill Mrs. Pembleton. I know you couldn't have killed Gomez, because you weren't even in Canfield when he was drugged and killed. Even if the coroner is wrong about the time of death, you aren't big enough to have drugged a man twice your size and hoisted him to the roof without so much as a step stool."

"Back up. Drugged?" DeLancey asked.

"With two of the pills Dr. Howard prescribed for you. They found traces in Gomez's blood samples. You're completely in the clear."

Her head dropped forward, and he watched as her shoulders heaved with silent sobs. "No, I'm not."

Matt felt his stomach drop into his shoes as he stood and gathered her in his arms. He told himself that at the very worst, DeLancey might have unwittingly helped Faircloth steal funds. "If you tell me the truth now, I can help you."

"I can't," she said, sobbing.

"If I can wake Dylan and Shelby to get your address at three in the morning knowing full well that Dylan—and maybe even Shelby—will probably punch me for also waking up two of the kids, then I think it's only proper for you to stick your neck out a bit, as well.''

DeLancey's sobs subsided, and she became very still and quiet. She asked him to sit on the sofa, then went to the window, moved one of the horizontal blinds and looked out on the small garden she had planted earlier in the summer. She tried not to think about what she would lose by confessing all. Instead, she focused on the knowledge that she was about to rid herself of a terrible secret.

"I didn't kill Mrs. Pembleton."

"I know."

"You already know that I arrived at the Tillman Plantation when I was fifteen. Well, I arrived without a memory."

"Excuse me?"

DeLancey stared out the window without seeing. "I simply opened my eyes, and I was blank. Well, not totally blank. There was nothing wrong with my cognitive skills, and believe me, Dr. Howard tested me a couple of times every month in the beginning.''

"You mean all your guilt and keeping people at arm's length is because you feel guilty about not being able to remember your childhood?'' he asked incredulously.

DeLancey turned and faced him. "Of course not. There's more."

"How much more can there be? You were only fifteen.''

She said, "When Gomez found me, I was covered in blood."

"You must have been in an accident. You wouldn't be the first person to sustain a head injury and go wandering."

"I also had a knife. A bloody one. In my pocket."

Matt didn't have a quick explanation for that one.

"Still want me to bare my soul?" she asked with self-loathing. "I'm not running because I want to. I have to, Matt. Don't you see?"

"Frankly, no."

"I killed someone, Matt."

He jumped to his feet. "You don't know that."

"What other explanation could there be?"

"Maybe you were attacked. Maybe you were covered in animal blood because you'd been homeless and hungry and you poached an animal for food."

"Then why don't I remember?" she shouted.

"Because your mind doesn't want you to."

She pressed her fingers to her temples. "You and Dr. Howard must have compared notes. He used to tell me that my mind was giving me a gift."

"Howard knows all this?"

"Some of it," DeLancey admitted. "Mrs. Pembleton had him treat me that first night."

"Treat you for what?"

"Stab wounds."

"Where?"

"My arms. Why?"

"Do you have scars?"

DeLancey nodded. "They're faint, but you can see them if you look closely."

Matt came over and examined the scars on the inside of her forearms as well as the smaller ones on her palm and in between two of the fingers of her left hand. "They could be defensive wounds, the kind of injuries we would see on victims who had struggled with their attackers."

She pulled her arm back. "I think you're trying to explain away the obvious just because we slept together."

His thumb traced her jawline before he gently forced her to meet his soft gray gaze. "I'm looking for explanations because I care about you."

"Please, Matt, don't say things like that. Now that you know the truth—"

"I don't know anything except that a fifteen-year-old injured girl was found in a cemetery during a rainstorm. The rest is pure conjecture on your part."

"Wishful thinking on your part," she countered. "C'mon, Matt. You were a cop. The only scenario that fits is—I killed someone, ran away and then blocked it out because of guilt and shame."

He sighed deeply, bathing her upturned face with his warm, minty breath. "How about this scenario? A fifteen-year-old girl gets attacked by someone—an angry stepfather, a boyfriend, whatever—fights him off, takes his weapon and runs. Perhaps she falls and hits her head. Then, dazed and still clutching the knife, she finds refuge from the rain in a cemetery."

"That doesn't explain the yellow room."

"What yellow room?"

"I have this flash. It's little more than a split second, just this picture, this image." She told him about the blood spattering on the floral curtains.

"That doesn't mean you killed anyone."

"Then why didn't anyone ever come looking for me?" she asked. "Mrs. Pembleton told the sheriff, and he told her there were no reports about a missing girl, nor had he gotten any alert on a murder."

Matt picked her up and spun her around. "That proves *my* point," he insisted. "If you had stabbed someone, there would have been a police circular on the crime. At the very worst, you could have injured someone. But the fact that no one pressed any charges goes a long way toward proving that whoever you tangled with had to be the aggressor."

She allowed a small ray of hope to pour into her. "You think so? I mean *really* think so?"

"You have nothing to lose if we investigate. I assume I'm the only one you've told this to."

She felt the hope drain from her body. "Someone else knows."

"Who?"

"Alan, I think."

"Alan's in jail. Why do you think he knows?"

"There was a picture in Mrs. P.'s bedroom. It disappeared about the time she died."

"With the envelope you told me about?"

She nodded. "Someone made an enlargement of it

on one of those color copiers and left it for me to find.''

''Where?''

''At DeLancey Jones's grave.''

He looked dumbfounded. ''Come again?''

''There's a crypt in the cemetery. When Gomez asked me my name that first night, I couldn't remember. I just read off the first inscription I came across.''

''You have no idea what your real name is?''

She shook her head sadly. ''I've been researching old murder cases trying to find one that fits my circumstances.''

Matt offered his dimpled grin. ''I guess that explains your interest. And I thought you were just morbid.''

''But I still don't understand why Alan would have put red paint all over the cemetery and taped the picture and the knife to the grave.''

''That's what spooked you yesterday?''

''Hell, yes! Wouldn't you get a little freaked if someone recreated one of your crime scenes?''

''Was it exact?''

''Excuse me?''

''Was it like the night you...''

''Woke up?'' she supplied. ''That was always Mrs. Pembleton's sanitary version of my mental state when she found me. But no, it wasn't exact. When Gomez found me, I had ditched the knife behind one of the headstones. It was a while before I told Mrs. Pembleton about it, and she had Gomez go get it. As far as I know, she destroyed it.''

"So Gomez and Mrs. Pembleton definitely knew, right?''

"Yes, and Alan, probably.''

"You don't know that, but it's a good guess. Even the new will stipulated that if you refused the inheritance, he would get what he wanted.''

DeLancey rested her cheek against his chest. "But I never would have guessed that Alan could do such a great job of disguising his voice.''

"You mean the call?'' Matt asked. "The raspy guy?''

"It didn't sound like Alan.''

"What about Dr. Howard?''

"He's known almost everything from the beginning. But I can't believe he would do anything to hurt me. He's always been very protective, and if he told anyone about me, he'd have to admit to his minor infraction of the law.''

"Which was?''

"Promise you won't tell on him?''

"Yes.''

"He filled out a phony birth certificate for me so I could enroll in school.''

"Was Mrs. Pembleton your legal guardian?''

DeLancey nodded. "We had to do that so I could live with her and go to school.''

"Who did the work? And how did it get done if no one knew your true identity?''

She shrugged. "I guess Alan took care of it. I was only fifteen, Matt. I only knew that a wonderful woman was bending the law to keep me out of jail or an orphanage. I wasn't exactly questioning her methods at the time."

"Then we have someplace to start," Matt suggested.

"Start what?"

"We're going to find out what happened ten years ago."

"I can't!" she yelled. "I know I should pay for my crime." The words came out of her mouth rapidly as she returned to pacing. "But I don't want to go to prison, Matt."

He caught her and pulled her to him. "I think it's a little early to be thinking about prison."

DeLancey winced. For almost the first time in their acquaintance, Matt hadn't said just the right thing. He said it was too early to think about prison, not that prison wouldn't happen. But despite her terror at the thought of paying for a crime she couldn't remember, DeLancey realized she was afraid of more than just prison. She was afraid of falling more in love with Matt Tanner. And it was happening. She couldn't help it. But she had to try.

"Will you promise me something?"

"If I can," he said.

"We can't sleep together again."

"Why not?"

"I just don't feel right about it."

"You felt fine a few hours ago, as I remember it."

DeLancey felt her cheeks burn. "That was when I didn't think I'd see you again."

"Thanks a lot." He let her go abruptly.

"I just don't think we should complicate our relationship until I know who I am."

There was a long pause before Matt grudgingly said, "Deal." He moved to the door. "I'm going to go to Dylan's and get some sleep."

"You can have the couch," she offered.

"I'll come back for you around ten, and we'll get started." He shook his head and flashed her a tired but sexy smile as he went to the door. "I'm a good sport, DeLancey, but I'm not interested in going from your bed to your couch."

Chapter Eleven

"It lives."

Matt gave his older brother a pointed glare. On his way to get his caffeine fix, he stopped long enough to scratch the dog's head. Foolish's tail thumped loudly against the floor as he waited for Matt to take his coffee to the table. Foolish was a great dog. Slip him a few doughnuts under the table and he was yours for life.

"It's nine o'clock," Dylan said.

"Are you the time fairy?" Matt snapped.

"No," Dylan replied easily. "I'm the guy you awakened from a peaceful sleep last night, or should I say this morning?"

Matt gave his brother a more forceful back-off glance. "I didn't have the best night of my life, either."

Dylan chuckled. "I figured that out when you came home. The lovely chef refused to share her kitchen?"

"The lovely chef's kitchen is none of your business."

"Whoops," Dylan said, punctuating the remark with a low whistle. "This *is* serious. I should have known you weren't looking for DeLancey's address in the middle of the night just to borrow a cup of sugar. Judging by your lack of sleep, generally lousy mood and those deep lines on your forehead, you, little brother, are in love."

"Don't gloat," Matt warned. "And I'm not sure I'm in love. DeLancey isn't exactly a one-dimensional woman."

"Then think of her as a challenge. You've always loved a challenge."

"A puzzle is more like it," Matt grumbled.

Dylan got the coffeepot to refill both their cups. "You've always been good at putting together puzzles. Except for when the rest of us would hide your pieces."

"I knew I would have been happier as an only child," Matt said without any real malice. "I'm tied up in knots eight ways from Wednesday and all you can do is joke and reminisce about what a lousy sibling you were."

"Tell me about it."

Matt blew out a breath of frustration. "I can't."

"I promise, no more jokes," Dylan said as he drew a cross over his heart. "What's the problem?"

"I really *can't* tell you," Matt said. "But you might be able to help me."

"Name it."

"Know anyone in the FBI who would do me a favor?"

"Define *favor*."

"I want to know if anything big happened around Canfield about ten years ago."

"Why?"

"I just need the information," he said. "Forget you're an ATF agent for ten minutes, remember you're my big brother and do me this favor. I'm not asking you to breach national security. I'm just asking you to pull a few strings for me."

"I'm assuming you want me to treat this as if it's part of your doctoral research?"

Matt nodded.

"Give me a few days, and I'll see what I can find out."

Let it be good news, Matt prayed silently.

IT WAS FIVE MINUTES before the hour when Matt climbed the stairs to DeLancey's apartment. A small part of his mind wondered if he'd find her there. *Maybe I should have taken her up on the couch idea.*

As he lifted his hand to knock, DeLancey opened the door and greeted him with a smile. It was the best he'd seen her look in days.

The smell of citrus clung to her freshly washed hair. He hated the way his eyes were drawn to where she held the edges of her terry-cloth robe together. Just that small hint of cleavage was enough to turn his thoughts to fantasies.

"Sorry," she murmured as she ushered him inside.

The boxes and suitcase were gone, and the apartment was in perfect order.

"I overslept," she explained.

"You must have worked until dawn," he commented. He watched the sensual sway of her hips as he followed her through the living room.

"I've got almond croissants in the oven. Do you mind keeping an eye on them while I throw some clothes on?"

He would have preferred to keep his eyes on her throughout that process, but he dutifully went into the small kitchen while she went into the bedroom.

Last night he hadn't really paid much attention to her apartment. Now he looked around and was struck instantly by the lack of personal items. Nothing hung on the walls unless he counted the hot pads hooked on a peg above the gas stove. He remembered that it had taken only two boxes and an equal number of suitcases for her to pack all her belongings from the Tillman estate. It appeared that DeLancey owned nothing in the world but clothing, a set of dishes minus the coffee cup she'd dropped earlier in the morning and some fancy cookware.

Carefully, he cracked the oven door and the scent of warm, buttery pastry and almonds filled the small kitchen. With one of the pot holders from the peg, Matt took the tray out of the oven and placed it on the stove. He shut off the gas, then went to the living room.

DeLancey appeared a few minutes later. A fitted cotton dress in a pale shade of lilac complemented her dark coloring. The dress caressed her thighs as she moved fluidly about the apartment. Her legs were toned, tanned and perfectly proportioned for her small frame. Her perfect shape made the plain dress look seductive.

"Ready to get started?" she asked.

"More than ready." He sighed, though he doubted they were discussing the same thing.

She went into the kitchen and slid a box from under the table. "This is everything I've collected so far."

She brought him the box, which contained neat file folders organized by date. "How many cases are here?"

"Twenty-three," she answered. "I've searched newspapers from the entire state of South Carolina. These are the only ones that coincided with the date Gomez found me in the cemetery and involved a stabbing."

Matt lifted the first file. It contained an article about a young man found stabbed in an alley in someplace called Summerville. "This was a fatal stabbing."

"They all are."

Matt glanced over as she sat next to him on the sofa. He wished her perfume wasn't so distracting. Hell, he wished for a whole lot more than that.

"What about nonfatal stabbings?"

A series of small lines appeared at the bridge of her nose when she frowned. "I've never really paid much attention to those. I've only researched murder."

Matt tapped his finger on the tip of her nose. "Mistake number one."

Her dark eyes narrowed. "I want your help, not condescension."

"Don't get into a snit," he remarked. "By looking for possible holes in your research, I *am* helping you."

"It feels more like criticism," she grumbled.

She went into the kitchen and started banging the metal tray that held the croissants. He grinned when he heard her abuse some plates, the water faucet and finally the coffeepot.

Forcing his attention to the files, Matt was impressed by how thoroughly she had compiled information. Unfortunately, most of her files culminated with a clipping that indicated the police had a suspect or suspects, and eventually a conviction.

He stacked the reports of the few cases that were unsolved on the table next to the box. "I take it none of these names are familiar to you?" he asked when she carried in pastry and coffee.

"Nope."

She set the food on the table, then thumbed through the files he had set aside. "This one," she said, tapping the folder, "involved an elderly couple who were stabbed in their home. The house was ransacked and all the jewelry and electronic equipment taken. Including a rear-projection wide-screen television."

"Something tells me an eighty-pound fifteen-year-old would be an unlikely possibility for that one. I just can't see you with a television strapped to your back."

DeLancey gave him a smart look. "I weighed eighty-five pounds, thank you very much."

"Where is Anderson?" he asked, scanning more articles.

DeLancey went into the kitchen, opened a drawer and returned with a map. She pointed to one of a dozen or so hand-drawn red circles. "Here," she said.

Matt glanced at the map. "That's a good hundred and fifty miles from Canfield. The bodies were discovered by a maid at noon. What time did you turn up in the cemetery?"

"It was late afternoon."

"Just for the sake of argument, let's say you had an accomplice who ransacked the house and took the valuables."

"Do we *have* to have an argument?"

"Quiet," he instructed as he processed the facts. "It would be nearly impossible for you to take a two hour drive and still have fresh blood on your clothing."

"What if the rain made it seem fresh?" DeLancey asked.

Hearing the catch of fear in her voice, Matt gave her shoulders a reassuring squeeze. "That's a remote possibility. Maybe it would be better if I went through this stuff by myself. I have a habit of thinking out loud when I'm reconstructing a crime.''

''No,'' she said firmly. ''I don't want you to shut me out of this. It's my life that's at stake, not yours.''

Reluctantly, he let his arm slip from her warm skin. ''What about this one?''

They continued well into the afternoon. Matt had narrowed the possibilities to two, one in Redbank and one in Pontiac. ''I think we should go up there and check out these towns. The clippings you have are vague and incomplete. The towns might have libraries with more information.''

''Go there?'' DeLancey asked in a voice filled with trepidation. The emotion was mirrored in her troubled eyes. ''But what if someone recognizes me?''

''It's been ten years,'' Matt reasoned. ''Tuck your hair under a cap and put on sunglasses if it will make you feel better.''

''Why do I have to go?''

''Because you're the only one of us who can identify the house with the yellow walls and floral curtains.'' He saw her shiver and cradled her to his side. ''I won't let anything happen to you.''

''I don't recall a big *S* on your chest. If someone recognizes me…''

He kissed her hair to reassure her. ''Do you want to drop it? Do you want to keep on living like this?''

''You make it sound like I don't have a life. I do. I've worked hard to make something of myself.''

"And you have," Matt insisted. "That's what I'm saying. Do you want to throw all that away?"

"No. I want to know the truth. But the truth scares me."

Matt held her tightly and thought, *Me, too.*

"I promised Joanna I would be at her office at five," DeLancey said.

"That's probably a very good idea." Especially if the worst became the reality. "Tell her everything, DeLancey."

"I'm not sure I can."

He turned, cupped her cheeks and forced her to meet his eyes. "You have to. You have to protect yourself, just in case." Her expression was apprehensive, and it tugged at his heart. He wanted to reassure her without lying to her. When his gaze dropped to her tremulous mouth, he began to dip his head.

"No," she said as she pressed her hands against his chest. "We have a deal, remember?"

He frowned. "I made that deal when I was exhausted from driving back roads for hours, followed by a frantic search for you. I think that counts as 'not of sound mind.'"

Her head tilted as she reached up and took his hands in her much smaller ones. She held them against her heart. "Look, as I said before, I'm not in any position to allow anything to start between us."

"I think we already passed the starting line when we made love."

"That shouldn't have happened," she insisted. "It was a foolish mistake."

"Not for me."

She searched his face, then said gently, "It was for me."

Her rejection hit him hard. Especially since her eyes completely repudiated her words. He left her apartment trying to understand why she was so intent on pushing him away when he didn't think that was what she wanted.

DELANCEY SET the car alarm after parking in the driveway of Joanna and Gabe's home. The first floor of Joanna's house served as her office. At least for now. According to Rose, the arrival of the baby had severely depleted their second-floor living space.

She went up the flower-lined walk and into the office. She was greeted by Joanna's secretary, who introduced herself as Tammy, then began shutting down the computer and locking her desk for the night. "She's on the phone, but she should be out in a minute."

"Thanks," DeLancey said over the lump of uneasiness clogging her throat.

Tammy slung her purse over one shoulder, told DeLancey the coffee was fresh, then slipped out.

Aside from the muffled sound of Joanna's voice filtering from beneath the closed door, the house was quiet. She guessed that was a blessing. She wasn't in a mood to make small talk with Gabe. He was a great guy, but in addition to being Joanna's devoted husband, he was a private detective and the son of her employer. She was in no great hurry to spread the details of her sordid past any further than she had to.

"How are you?" Joanna greeted her as she twisted her unruly red hair into a knot at the nape of her neck. Frowning, she added, "You look like hell."

DeLancey managed a half smile. "Obviously you and Rose have compared notes. She isn't too impressed with my looks, either."

"Come on in."

Joanna sat quietly and without judgment as DeLancey told her almost everything. She left out only her seduction of Matt and her thwarted plan to flee Charleston.

"No wonder you didn't want to take a polygraph," Joanna said with feeling. "Alan Faircloth's arrest should make that a moot point."

"That arrest still doesn't make any sense to me," DeLancey said. Telling her story for the second time in twenty-four hours was taking its toll.

"You said he was a greedy creep."

"Land greedy," DeLancey insisted. "He wanted the Tillman Plantation. His mother and Mrs. Pembleton were second cousins. They were the only Tillmans left. Alan considered the estate his birthright."

"He probably just got tired of waiting to inherit and decided to hurry things along. I can have Gabe check—"

"No!" DeLancey recovered and repeated the word

in a more reasonable tone. "I don't want to involve Gabe or Rose."

Joanna was clearly affronted. "I'm required to keep your confidences, DeLancey. Gabe may be my husband and Rose's son, but neither one of us would ever do anything in violation of client privilege."

"I know," DeLancey said apologetically. "But I'm more interested in finding out what happened ten years ago. Maybe once I know that, I'll understand how Alan could do this."

"What if he didn't do it?"

DeLancey's shoulders slumped. "Then I guess the police will focus on me again."

"No one else had motive? What about—" she paused and consulted her notes. "Stephen Thomason? Or Dr. Howard?"

"Alan hired Stephen about a year ago. Mrs. Pembleton liked him, and it seemed to me like the feeling was mutual."

"Do you know anything about him?"

"He's one of those brownnosing types. Humble words and hot air. But harmless, I think. Besides, he had nothing to gain by Mrs. Pembleton's death."

"There's the missing money," Joanna suggested.

"But Alan had power of attorney, not Stephen."

"What about the doctor?"

DeLancey shook her head and spoke vehemently. "No way."

"You're sure?"

"Positive. I always had the impression that he and

Mrs. Pembleton went way back. Besides, he's a doctor. If he wanted to kill her, I'm sure he could have come up with something more imaginative and less easily detected than rat poison.''

"Unless he was intentionally trying to put suspicion on you or Gomez.''

"He's also in his eighties,'' DeLancey said. "According to Matt, Gomez was drugged and unconscious when he was killed. Dr. Howard isn't strong enough to lift Gomez and put a noose around his neck.'' DeLancey rubbed her suddenly chilled arms. "Gomez weighed at least two hundred pounds.''

"Let's get to the call you got after you found the gory little scene in the cemetery.''

A shiver crawled up her spine. "All I can tell you is that it was a man's voice.''

"Have you ever been threatened before?''

DeLancey shook her head. "Never. In fact, there was an unwritten rule at Tillman. No one ever brought up the details of how or when I was found.''

"Are you sure Faircloth handled the guardianship?''

"No.''

"I'll check the court records and let you know.''

"Thanks,'' DeLancey said. "I might be in and out, but I'll try to let your secretary know where to find me.''

Joanna offered a comforting smile. "We'll get you through this.''

"I hope so," DeLancey whispered as she left the office.

She disarmed her car with the button on her key-chain from about twenty feet away. Her legs felt like stone, and her mind was numb.

She drove to her apartment replaying Joanna's questions in her mind.

"Maybe I'm missing something," she mused. *Something besides Matt.* "Stop it!" she commanded the errant voice in her head. Still, she couldn't think of a single explanation that could tie her past to the present murders. "Unless this is about revenge." She sighed. Maybe someone connected to the person or people she had murdered was seeking his or her own brand of justice. Maybe Mrs. P. and Gomez had been killed to even a ten-year-old score.

Sluggishly, she climbed the stairs to her apartment. It was a painful thought.

DeLancey reached for the doorknob and stopped. Staring at the gruesome sight before her, she screamed and stumbled toward the rickety wooden railing.

Chapter Twelve

"Did you see anyone in the building as you were coming upstairs?" Matt demanded as he took the knife and the copy of the picture from her. "Too bad you handled it, but the police can still test it for prints."

She took the picture and slammed it facedown on the table. "I'm glad you thought I should have left it tacked to the front door. What if one of my neighbors saw it? Besides, we can't call the police."

Matt felt his ire rise. "Why the hell not? Some jerk hung your picture on the door with a knife through your forehead. A rational person would see that as the threat it is, not blame *you* for it!"

She glared at him. "I'm *being* rational. If I call the police, how do you propose I explain this to them?"

"You're good at evasion."

"Forgive me, Professor, but if I could manage to create a story to explain the picture and the knife, wouldn't I have to give my fingerprints for a comparison?"

Matt felt his shoulders fall as he let out a breath. ''Yes, you would have to be excluded as a suspect, since you touched the stuff.''

When he saw DeLancey's small body trembling, he reached out and pulled her into his arms. ''I'm sorry I came on so strong. I just don't like the idea that some nutcase is out there.''

Her arms went around his waist. ''It's worse than you think.''

''How?''

''It's the same picture and knife I saw in the cemetery.''

''At least there wasn't any red paint this time,'' Matt said in an attempt to lighten the mood.

''I wish there had been.''

''Why?''

''The paint wasn't half as scary as knowing whoever is doing this knows where I live.''

''Not for long,'' Matt said. ''Pack whatever you need. We're getting out of here.''

''And going where?''

''I'll work on that while you get packed,'' he said as he turned her toward the bedroom door.

DeLancey emerged a few minutes later with a small bag over her shoulder. ''Have you figured out where I'm going to hide?''

''Yep. In plain sight.''

She gaped at him. ''You want me to stay here?''

''Nope. We're going to Canfield.''

''Why?''

"To get some answers."

"I looked for answers in Canfield for ten years," DeLancey insisted. "They aren't there."

He draped his arm over her shoulder and led her from the apartment. "Maybe you haven't looked in the right places."

"You aren't making sense."

He waited at the landing while she locked the apartment. "Whoever is making copies of the picture and trying to drive you crazy has to be the person who took the picture from Mrs. Pembleton's dresser."

"That's a short list."

"Maybe," Matt said. "There were a lot of people in the house when they took her to the hospital. But there's also the matter of why Alan Faircloth didn't tell the sheriff all about you when he was arrested. If he arranged for your guardianship, then he must know DeLancey Jones isn't your real name."

She nodded. "You're right. Alan has absolutely no reason to protect me."

"We'll take two cars," he said. When DeLancey hesitated he explained. "I want it to be blatantly obvious that you're at the house."

"Why does that make me feel like bait?"

"Because you will be." He brushed her open mouth with a light kiss. "But well-protected bait."

MATT FOUND the drive completely uneventful except when he passed the bare spot on the shoulder of the road where he and DeLancey had shared that incredible kiss. "What are you getting yourself in to?" he asked himself for the umpteenth time. If he had a brain, he'd be organizing material for his thesis, not involving himself with a woman who had no past.

"Unless you consider the way she was found," he mumbled as the wind whipped through his hair. He looked ahead to DeLancey's sedan. Her distant silhouette alone was enough to make his heart turn over. "You're hooked," he admitted. "Great work, Tanner. You finally fall in love, and the woman may or may not be a fugitive." He laughed without humor. There was something really perverse about this. But nothing was as perverse as what was being done to DeLancey. His cop's instincts told him that disaster was on the horizon. And his apprehension deepened as they reached Tillman Plantation. Matt parked in the shadows of a low-hanging oak.

He reached the steps while DeLancey was digging in her purse for the key to the front door. He had his bag in one hand and grabbed DeLancey's bag, as well.

"We forgot something," she said as they walked in.

"Not if the weight of your bag is any indication."

"Very funny. They removed all the food for testing after Mrs. P. died. There's nothing here I can turn into dinner."

"It's late," Matt said. "Neither one of us had much sleep last night. Isn't there someplace in Canfield where we could grab a bite to eat?"

DeLancey looked uneasy. "This is a really small town," she reminded him.

He took her hand and said, "Who cares? I can handle it. I've been stared at a time or two."

"I'll bet."

Matt laughed as he led her out of the house. "Thank you."

"For what?"

"Your sharp-edged compliment."

"It was an observation, not a compliment."

He made sure she was safely in his car, then got behind the wheel. "Keep trying, DeLancey. We both know it was your roundabout way of telling me you think I'm cute."

"Your kind-person façade is slipping," DeLancey warned him teasingly. "You're turning into that egotistical man who haunted me relentlessly for more than a month."

He gave her a wink. "It worked."

"Hardly. The luncheonette is on the left side of Main Street."

"It *did* work. We're together, aren't we?"

"Logistically," she retorted. "We have a deal in place."

Matt was smiling as he escorted DeLancey into the diner. "You're welcome to pretend you have no feelings for me. I know better. I'll be patient—for a while."

"You're pressuring me, Professor," she said as she slipped into a booth.

Matt sat opposite her and reached for a menu from behind ketchup and mustard bottles. He passed one to her.

"DeLancey Jones!"

Matt looked up and saw a slightly familiar blue-haired lady moving toward them.

"Great," DeLancey mumbled with a forced smile. "Get ready, Miss Foster is on a mission."

"The flirty lady with the old pickup we met the first day here?"

"The one and only."

"I heard you were in town," Miss Foster said as she slipped into the booth, scrunching DeLancey into the corner. "I can't believe Esther is gone. That other one, too. Gopher?"

"Gomez," DeLancey corrected.

The woman smiled in Matt's general direction. "We haven't seen this much murder and mayhem in Canfield before."

"You're talking about my friends," DeLancey said gently but with meaning.

Miss Foster had the decency to look properly chastened. But not for very long. "Of course they were, dear. And you must be furious at what Judge Lang did."

"Judge Lang?" Matt queried.

"He dismissed the case against Alan Faircloth last night. Said something about no direct evidence."

Matt could almost hear DeLancey's mind whirl. "Let's get something to go," he suggested. DeLancey seemed grateful for his suggestion. In fact, for a minute there, he thought she might climb over the table to get away from the old gossip.

Miss Foster hung around while they ordered and waited for sandwiches to be prepared. She filled them in on every whispered rumor making its way around town. As Matt was collecting their order, Miss Foster mentioned there had been talk that perhaps DeLancey was involved. "But I know better," she added quickly. "I know that sweet young girl who used to bake my cakes couldn't possibly do harm to Esther or Gopher."

"Gomez," DeLancey repeated.

"I'm more inclined to believe it was Mr. Faircloth. Even as a boy, he couldn't stand the fact that he was a poor relation. I remember how he used to stand in the road and stare at the farm from the wrong side of the fence."

"Thanks," DeLancey said. "We've got to go."

DELANCEY HELD the lunch bag in her lap as they drove out of the parking lot under the watchful eye of Miss Foster. "She must have a telescope on her roof."

"I wouldn't be surprised." Matt chuckled.

She turned and took in his angled profile. Her brain must be dulled from lack of sleep. That was the only reason she could give for allowing herself to admire his handsome, chiseled features. She should be thinking productive thoughts, solving the crime, unraveling the mystery of her past, not remembering how heavenly it was to be in Matt's arms.

"You're quiet," he said. "Is it because Faircloth is on the loose?"

"No, I was just thinking."

"About what?"

She was too tired to pretend. "Remembering what it was like to have sex with you."

"I'm willing to remind you," he said as his hand slipped temptingly up her thigh.

With an effort, DeLancey removed it. "I was remembering it, not suggesting we do it."

"That isn't exactly a comfort to me. Especially considering the fact that your celibacy rule wasn't my idea."

"Put your testosterone away," she said. "We agreed we wouldn't complicate things until we had some answers."

"Great. Care to tell me why you felt the need to share your dirty thoughts?"

"It feels good not to have to lie anymore."

"I think I'd rather have you lie to me. It would make things easier."

"Okay. When it comes to sex, I'll remember to lie in the future."

"Or we could stop pretending we don't want each other."

"What makes you think I'm pretending?" she quipped.

"You're the one who brought up sex, not me."

"For the last time, if you'd listen with your ears instead of your hormones, you would hear that I was reminiscing, not planning."

"You know something?" Matt asked as he pulled into his secret parking place. "If we keep discussing this topic, I'll be forced to change your mind about being together."

"It won't happen," she promised as she bounded from the car. "I have strength and self-control on my side."

"Oh, really?" Matt taunted as he followed her in.

"That's the difference between men and women, Professor. Women have a much better ability to control themselves."

"Let's test that theory," he said.

In a flash, Matt had taken the bag from her, placed it on the counter and had her back against the kitchen wall. He looked at her with smoldering gray eyes.

"I'm going to eat, take a bath and get some sleep," she announced.

"Not until we settle this."

Though her insides were melting, her convictions remained intact. "It is settled. Can we eat now? Or would you like to continue roughing me up?"

"I'm not roughing you up," Matt said.

DeLancey smiled sweetly. "No, but you'd probably like to."

Matt stepped away from her and jammed his hands into the front pockets of his jeans. "For someone who needs my help, you sure are tweaking my last nerve."

"It isn't your nerve I tweak," she said as she stepped past him, "and we both know it."

"Keep pushing," he warned softly.

"The only appetite of yours I'll satisfy right now is this one," she said as she tossed one of the sandwiches directly at his broad chest.

Matt's reflexes were fast. His hand was out of his pocket long before her off-center throw hit the target. "Beer, wine, coffee, soda?"

"Wine."

She uncorked a bottle of Chablis, grabbed some glasses and joined him at the table.

"You're forgetting your sandwich," he observed.

"I'm on a liquid diet," she quipped as she poured a generous amount of wine for them both.

"Not healthy."

"Not open for discussion," she retorted with a smile. "I'm too tired to eat." She watched him devour the sandwich in just a few bites. "A concept I see is foreign to you."

"I'm a big boy," he said before taking a sip of wine.

"Not always."

Matt got a devilish glint in his eye. "Are we talking about my appetite or my—"

"Don't go there," she warned, taking another sip of wine. "I'm going to sleep."

"I'll walk you up," Matt offered.

His simple gesture inspired quite a response from her overloaded senses. She'd been teasing him, hoping that if they kept talking, some of the electricity that drew her to him would dissipate. However, as they moved toward the steps, she was keenly aware of his fluid movements. Her shoulder brushed his solid chest, inciting a whole new array of thoughts and feelings.

When he placed his fingers at the small of her back, DeLancey couldn't ignore the warmth of his touch. She tried to convince herself it was just a reaction caused by her recent traumas. But the masculine scent she had grown to associate with him caressed her senses and weakened her resistance.

"Are you afraid to be in this house? I really don't think Faircloth has the guts to come at you without a plan," he said when they reached the door to her bedroom. "Besides, I'm going to take the front bedroom. The way these floorboards creak, I'll have plenty of warning."

DeLancey looked into his eyes. He was so tall, his shoulders so broad that she could feel her pulse begin to quicken. "I feel safe here. I have since I was fifteen."

One ebony brow arched and his mouth curved into a lazy smile. "It makes perfect sense to me. Besides, unless Miss Foster went running to Faircloth, it should be tomorrow before anyone knows we're here."

"True," she acknowledged softly.

He rested one hand on her shoulder near her collarbone. She could feel every inch of his squared fingers. But intoxicating as it was, his touch wasn't nearly as powerful as the simmering passion she saw in those sexy, darkening gray eyes of his.

DeLancey felt her breath catch in her throat as the air between them grew thick. It was as if the current had engaged, filling the inches that separated them with a strong and powerful electricity. For several protracted seconds they said nothing. DeLancey was afraid of breaking the magic. She didn't know what might happen, but she did know that the budding bond between them made her feel connected and alive.

His eyes traveled lower, until she could almost feel him staring hard at her slightly parted lips. She knew Matt's thoughts were taking the same path as her own. His hand moved slowly toward her face and he cupped her cheek, his thumb resting just inches from where his eyes remained riveted.

His thumb burned a path toward her lower lip. She watched the intensity in his eyes deepen as his thumb brushed tentatively across her mouth. She told herself that she could stop this at any time. He was gentle at first, then with each successive movement he applied more pressure until DeLancey thought she might die from the anticipation knotting her stomach.

Raising her hand, she flattened it against his chest. She could feel his heart beating under the solid muscle. A faint moan rumbled in his throat.

His head dipped fractionally closer, and she held her breath, fully expecting and wanting his kiss. His thumb continued to work its magic. The friction produced heat that was carried to every cell in her body. DeLancey swallowed words of protest.

"That first night," he began in a husky, raspy voice.

"Yes?"

"It was the most incredible thing I've ever experienced."

"Me, too."

"I'm glad."

His breath washed over her face in warm, inviting waves, but he did not move closer. Gathering a handful of his shirt, DeLancey urged him to her. His resistance was a surprise. His thumb stilled and rested just below her lip.

His eyes met and held hers. "I won't violate the deal without an invitation." Matt pulled her against him, cradling her head in his hand. She could feel and hear his heartbeat. "If you want me, DeLancey, you're going to have to ask me."

The first stirrings of embarrassment crept into her consciousness. She felt her face grow warm with the realization of how much she wanted him.

"Look," she said, stepping out of his arms with her head bowed. "I need a good night's sleep. Thanks for getting me out of Charleston and bringing me here. I don't know how I'll ever be able to thank you enough."

"I can think of a way," he answered before he turned and started down the hall.

She closed the door, leaned against the cool wooden surface and fanned herself with her hand. "Close," she mumbled. "Very close."

My car! DeLancey opened the door and had taken a step before Matt turned and looked at her questioningly. "I forgot to set my car alarm," she explained.

"I'll do it. Where are your keys?"

"In the kitchen. I can do it."

Matt shook his head. "I'll do it. You go to sleep."

"Thanks."

"DeLancey?" he said. There was a devilish glint in his eyes. "Ten bucks says you dream about me."

She offered a snooty smile. "Be prepared to pay up in the morning."

Trailing soft laughter, Matt went down the stairs as DeLancey returned to her room. When she saw the giddy smile on her face as she passed the dresser mirror, she decided she liked it. Matt made her feel alive. Matt made her feel connected. Matt made her—

The explosion threw her to the ground.

Chapter Thirteen

"Matt!" she called frantically, running down the stairs. The acrid scent of burning rubber and thick, dark smoke filled the foyer. "Matt!" she repeated when she saw him lying facedown on the floor.

The fire raging in the driveway seemed unimportant as she hurried through the smoke to kneel at his side. "Matt?" she said more softly. He didn't move.

It was a struggle, but she managed to roll him to his back. He groaned, which was a relief. He was alive.

He didn't appear to be burned, though the smell of burned hair was pungent. A rather large knot was swelling on his forehead. He started to cough, and moaned again.

Her eyes tearing from the smoke, DeLancey raced to the kitchen and dialed the emergency squad. Then she opened the back door to try to clear some of the smoke before racing to Matt.

He was trying to sit up.

"Stay still," she commanded as she got on her

knees and pulled his head into her lap. "I've called the paramedics."

"Not…necessary," he croaked as he brought his arm up and covered his eyes, his face frozen with pain.

DeLancey felt helpless. *Think!* "I'll get some ice for your head."

Matt said nothing but reached back to grasp her wrist. "I'll stay here," she amended as she wiped the perspiration from his forehead.

Matt's moans came less often. She looked up when she heard the approach of sirens. It was only then that she realized what had happened. Her car, or what was left of it, was burning. Bright orange flames and dark, swirling smoke were everywhere. She thought one of the car doors was in the center of the front yard, still smoldering.

The fire department went to work as the paramedics came up the steps.

"We need you to get out of the way," one of the young men said. He gently took her arm while his partner slipped a support beneath Matt's head.

She stepped back and wrung her hands as she watched them shine lights in his eyes and monitor his vital signs. One of the men left and returned carrying a backboard.

"I'm fine," Matt insisted as he shrugged the technicians aside.

The paramedics argued for ten minutes but got nowhere. If he didn't already have a lump on his head,

DeLancey might have given him one for being so stupid.

"You should let them take you to the hospital," she nagged, letting him lean on her as they went into the dining room, where the smoke and noise were greatly reduced. "You lost consciousness. You—"

"Give it a rest," he groaned. "I'm fine."

"You're dense, ' she said without malice. "Refusing medical treatment is dumb."

"I'm fine," he said more forcefully as he gave her his dimpled, innocent smile. "A glass of water would be great, though."

DeLancey got him the water. "Take small sips."

He laughed at her. "Nurse Jones?"

She let out an exasperated sigh. "Fine. Drink it in one swallow and choke. I don't care."

"Yes, you do," he teased. "You practically flew down those stairs to offer aid and comfort."

She waved him off. "Knee-jerk reaction. Surprise, that's all it was. I've never had to deal with a blown-up man in my foyer."

"Miss Jones?"

DeLancey looked up and saw Sheriff Beltram. Seeing him in the house brought all her defenses into place.

"Are you folks able to tell me what happened?"

"My car exploded," DeLancey said.

"I figured that out already," the sheriff said. "I was hoping you could give me some additional information."

"I went to set the alarm, and the car blew up," Matt said. "Someone obviously rerouted the circuitry so the alarm would detonate the bomb. Judging by the smell, I'd say it was made of fertilizer and diesel fuel."

The sheriff cocked one thick eyebrow. "You some sort of demolitions expert?"

Matt held the glass of ice water to the knot on his head. "New York City police, retired."

"Why would someone want to blow up your car?" the sheriff asked DeLancey.

"I think they were trying for me," she said. "Maybe someone who had their charges dismissed by Judge Lang?"

The sheriff colored but kept his anger in check. "I can't control the judge."

"But Alan can, right?"

The sheriff shrugged noncommittally. "Did you see anyone around the car?"

"No."

"Had any threats lately?"

DeLancey gave him a pointed look. "You mean other than the fact that the two people who lived here have been murdered recently?"

"DeLancey," Matt warned softly as he reached out and covered her hand. "Did you set the alarm in Charleston?"

"Not since I left Joanna's. I set it and disarmed it then."

"What time was that?" the sheriff asked.

"About five," she said. She shivered, then said, "I drove up here after that. I can't believe I drove a car rigged with a bomb for almost two hours."

"Unless it was rigged here," Matt suggested. He looked at the sheriff. "We went to the diner."

"He means the luncheonette," DeLancey corrected. "We were only gone about forty-five minutes."

"It doesn't take long to rig a fertilizer bomb if you know what you're doing," the sheriff observed, shaking his head.

"Don't you need special training?" she asked.

"You need the Internet," he said with disgust. "There's lots of sickos who think there is nothing wrong with listing the ingredients for a homemade bomb."

"That's sad."

"I can see you are both shaken up," the sheriff said. "I'd appreciate it if you could stop down to my office tomorrow."

"No problem," Matt answered for them both.

"No problem if you're you," DeLancey said when the sheriff was gone. "Big problem if you're me."

"I don't think he wants us to come in so he can grill you about Gomez and Mrs. Pembleton. It's pretty clear that someone wants to hurt you. He's trying to help, DeLancey."

"I hope you're right."

"YOUR FOREHEAD has one heck of a big bruise," DeLancey said by way of greeting when Matt came into the kitchen the next morning.

"Really? I wonder what could have caused it," he teased. "Sleep well?"

"No, I kept checking on you."

"And I enjoyed it," he said as he got himself some coffee. "By the way, you do great things for a pair of running shorts and a skimpy shirt. *Much* nicer than your average uniform."

DeLancey glared even as she felt herself blush. "You should sleep in more than just boxer shorts."

"If I'd known you were going to peek under the sheets, I wouldn't have worn a thing."

Flustered, she said, "I just moved the blanket back so I could see your chest."

Matt winked at her and leaned against the counter. "My chest is up here. That isn't where you were looking."

"How would you know?" she asked, more than a little mortified. "You were asleep."

He shook his head as a slow, knowing grin curved his mouth. "No, I wasn't. I was pretending."

"Why would you do that?"

He shrugged without a hint of remorse. "So I could smell your perfume and feel your body rub against mine every time you checked on my forehead."

DeLancey lowered her eyes. "I'm starting to remember why I didn't like you."

"You like me."

"Not when you're being an arrogant jerk."

"Are you always this testy in the morning?"

"Only when I have to suffer lousy company before my second cup of coffee."

Matt chuckled. "I'll remember that. Just like I'll remember the sweet way you ran your fingers over my chest last—"

"Enough," she said emphatically. "Why don't you—" The shrill of the phone interrupted her. She answered it.

"Hi, it's Dylan. Is my brother there?"

She looked at Matt and grinned. "Yes. Please tell me it's time for him to come home."

Dylan laughed. "Hey, possession is nine-tenths of the law. He's all yours."

"Hang on," she said as she passed Matt the phone. "It's someone who actually likes you."

Matt playfully swatted her on the behind as she left the kitchen. "What's up?" he asked.

"You've got a package waiting at the post office. It was too thick for the box."

"I'd run it past the bomb squad."

"Why?" Dylan asked, all traces of humor vanishing.

Matt explained about the car bomb.

"I'll have it checked at the office. If you want me to, I can send it to you if it comes out clean."

"Who's it from?"

"According to the note the mail carrier left, it's from the Carolina Military Academy," Dylan replied.

"You planning on switching to teaching little soldiers?"

"I was there a while back, gave one of the little generals a business card," he explained. "I wrote your address on the back of some of them, so it's probably run-of-the-mill catalog stuff. But be careful, bro. I couldn't stand it if you or your family—"

"Not to worry," Dylan said. "You watch your back. Want me to contact the field office up there?"

"Not yet," he said. "How about that information I asked for? Any leads?"

"Nothing yet," Dylan said. "Should I put the squeeze on my friend?"

"If you can."

"You're scaring me, Matt. What are you getting yourself into?"

"Don't know yet."

"Is this about DeLancey?"

"Don't know that, either. I'll be in touch."

At midmorning, Matt and DeLancey went to the sheriff's office. It wasn't Mayberry, but it wasn't modern, either. Matt placed his hand on DeLancey's back as they were shown in.

"You were right," the sheriff said to Matt without preamble. Opening a file from the top of a stack, he said, "Fertilizer and fuel. The state lab boys found where someone had tapped into the car's electrical system to detonate."

Matt nodded. "Fast work."

In response, the sheriff seemed less defensive,

which was exactly why Matt had given him the compliment. He needed Beltram on his side.

The sheriff sat holding the folder but not looking at it. His attention was focused on DeLancey. She was twisting her hair and withering under the officer's intent gaze.

"We've been wondering." Matt spoke to try to ease the situation. "Did you speak to Alan Faircloth last night?"

The sheriff looked at him and nodded. "He was in his home in Columbia. The state police questioned him, searched his house and his garage. His Mercedes runs on diesel, but we didn't find any fertilizer."

"I can't imagine Faircloth was too happy about that," Matt said in a commiserating tone.

"Fit to be tied," the sheriff replied. "He ranted and raged about everything from harassment to a huge civil suit against the town."

"How can we help?" Matt asked as he casually reached for DeLancey's trembling hand. "We do want to help, don't we, DeLancey?"

"Sure," she said, punctuating her answer by digging her fingernails into his palm. "That's why we came to see you today."

"Miss Jones, have you thought of anything that might explain why someone would want to hurt you?"

She shook her head. "Nothing."

"What about that story you told me?" Matt prompted.

She gave him a questioning look.

"You know. There was some sort of trouble one summer. What was it? Ten years ago?" Ignoring her wide, horrified eyes, Matt turned to the sheriff and said, "Mrs. Pembleton made a report to this office. Maybe if you found the old file, there could be a link."

"I can't remember answering a call out to the Tillman place. I can go see if there's anything in the computer. Do you know when the report was filed?"

Matt elbowed DeLancey and squeezed her hand until she finally said, "Summertime. Ten years ago. On July twenty-ninth."

He braced himself when Beltram left them alone. It was a good thing. DeLancey stood and glared at him with betrayal and anger in her eyes. "What the hell are you doing? You're going to get me arrested!"

Ignoring her hysterics, he said, "Go watch the door. Let me know what Beltram is coming back."

"Why should I—"

"Shut up and do it!" he commanded in a harsh whisper.

Matt quickly went through the files on the sheriff's desk. He found the one he was looking for close to the top. He managed to read most of it before De-Lancey signaled that the sheriff was coming.

"I hope you die," she whispered.

"No, you don't."

Beltram came in, glanced around and sat. "Are you sure about the date?"

"Uh…"

"She wasn't when she told me," Matt interrupted. Giving DeLancey a quick, silent warning, he smiled and said, "I could have sworn you told me it was winter."

"Could have been," DeLancey acquiesced. "Could have been fifteen years ago. Mrs. Pembleton wasn't always good on details," she said.

"I'll keep looking," the sheriff said. "But I can't see how some disturbance at the estate at least a decade ago could have any bearing on what's going on now."

Matt nodded. "I'm sure you're right, Sheriff." He rose and gave the man an enthusiastic handshake. "We'll keep thinking and let you work the case."

"That's always best," the sheriff said as he stood. "Don't you worry, Miss Jones. We've got Faircloth under surveillance. As soon as we can connect him to the fertilizer, we'll have him back in custody like that!" The sheriff snapped his fingers.

"I can't begin to tell you what coming here today has done for me," she said sweetly. "I'm just sorry I can't be more helpful. Goodbye for now."

"You take care now."

In the parking lot, Matt leaned close to her ear and said, "You can be very charming when you bat your lashes and pretend to be a nice, subservient Southern belle."

"As soon as we're away from the watchful eye of the sheriff, I'm going to show you charming."

Matt chuckled at her display of temper. He chuckled again when she refused to look at him in the car. "You should be thrilled, not pouting."

"I don't pout."

"No, you don't pay attention."

"Right," she said, scoffing. "What did I miss back there? You reading files? No. I caught that. Perhaps you're referring to the ruse you used to get the sheriff to leave his office. Geez, Matt! If you keep sucking up to him, maybe he'll let *you* slap the cuffs on my wrists."

"I was being polite, not sucking up. Though it would be nice if you gave either of those options a try."

"Oh, I *really* feel like being polite to you. What if the sheriff had found the file right away? Your little act could have landed me in an interrogation room trying to explain how I mysteriously appeared at the cemetery."

Matt shrugged. "It was a calculated risk, but it worked."

"What was so important in those files? Do you know what your little stunt has done? It's only a matter of time before Beltram finds the file and discovers I'm a fraud. He wouldn't even be looking for it if it wasn't for you!"

"Finished?" Matt asked as he pulled onto the shoulder.

"Thanks to you."

"You should be thanking me."

"For insuring Beltram reviews my past?"

"No," he said as he turned to look at her. "I insured that Beltram won't review your past."

"I gave him the date and everything."

Matt smiled. "And what did he turn up?"

"Nothing, yet."

"And he won't."

"How can you be sure?"

"I wasn't completely sure until we convinced him to look for a file."

"I'm confused."

"Beltram didn't find anything because there wasn't anything to find."

"But Mrs. Pembleton—"

"Lied about making a report to the sheriff."

Chapter Fourteen

"Why would she have lied?" DeLancey asked. It was almost impossible for her to believe Mrs. Pembleton had been anything but honest with her.

"I don't know. Maybe you're a distant relative. Maybe she was a lonely old woman who wanted company."

DeLancey fell onto the settee. "She wasn't like that. When she took me in, she was still active in the community. It wasn't like she was some desolate shut-in."

Matt walked around the room. Judging by the deep lines around his mouth, she assumed he was as confused as she was.

"Okay, you said Dr. Howard treated you, right? And he forged a birth certificate for you."

"You're suggesting Dr. Howard and Mrs. Pembleton conspired to keep me here for some unknown reason."

"Unknown now," Matt said. "But we can rectify that by paying the doctor a little visit."

DeLancey leaned her head back and closed her eyes, unable to accept that Mrs. P. and Dr. Howard had been complicit in some grand deception. "There has to be a logical explanation for this."

"Not really," Matt insisted as he knelt in front of her and took her hands. "Hear me out, DeLancey. I read most of Alan's statements to the police. He never once mentioned that you had no memory when he arranged the guardianship for Mrs. Pembleton. I don't think he even knew."

"So she never told him I had amnesia? I was fifteen. I have no idea what she told her attorney to do."

"Are you sure *you* never told Alan? Maybe something slipped out."

She shook her head. "It wasn't exactly as though we discussed it over tea. Maybe Alan just didn't mention it to the police."

"Would he avoid mentioning something like that? I don't think so. He would have ratted you out in a New York minute if he thought it would get his butt out of the sling. He also passed his polygraph."

She met his eyes. "I thought they weren't admissible in court."

"They aren't, but most police agencies use them as an investigative tool. From what I've seen of Alan, he doesn't have enough control over his temper to beat the machine. His face turns beet red when he's pressed. One of the things a polygraph machine measures is blood pressure."

"If Alan didn't kill Mrs. Pembleton and Gomez,

are you honestly suggesting that Dr. Howard is behind all this?''

"I'm not discounting Alan completely. I'm just saying I'm open to other suggestions. You tell me the name of anyone else who knows about your past. Anyone.''

DeLancey took a deep, calming breath. "So, what do we do now?''

"We see if the doctor is in.''

DeLancey followed Matt past the charred grass to his car. "I still don't understand why Dr. Howard would help Mrs. Pembleton do something illegal. Or how he would kill two people and steal money out of a trust fund he didn't have access to, then frame Alan by using his office equipment.''

"He faked a birth certificate.''

"Faking a birth certificate isn't arson and murder and theft,'' she reminded him. "How did he manage to steal from Mrs. Pembleton's accounts?''

"Good point. Tonight I might take a little stroll through Alan's office.''

"For what?''

"I'll know it when I see it.''

"That's comforting,'' DeLancey said. She directed Matt to Dr. Howard's office.

Like Joanna, Dr. Howard used a portion of his home as an office. The old Victorian house was beautifully maintained. It was something of a landmark in Canfield. As far back as DeLancey could recall, people had always commented on how Dr. Howard kept the elaborately painted trim looking fresh and the formal gardens manicured.

A small wooden sign with the doctor's name swayed in the early-afternoon breeze. "We have to go around back," she told Matt.

A worn fieldstone path wound through flowering hedges to the entrance. She opened the screen, then the door, which made a bell ring.

"Dr. Howard?" she called.

"Back here! Is that you, DeLancey?" he asked as he emerged, working an arm into the sleeve of his suit coat. "I was just on my way out to see patients." He smiled at her. "Miss Foster was here this morning to get her cholesterol checked and told me about your car. I was planning on looking in on you both."

"We're fine."

"Mr. Tanner, that bump on your head looks a little menacing."

Matt touched it as if he'd forgotten it was there. "It's not as bad as it looks."

The doctor took his medical bag off a chair. "I'd love to visit with the two of you," he said amiably, "not that Miss Foster didn't provide me with a full account of the fire. But I do need to make my rounds."

"This is important," Matt insisted.

"Oh," the doctor said with a nod. "I should have realized you had other injuries. Come into my examining room, Mr. Tanner."

"It isn't about my injuries," Matt said. "It's about

your not contacting the police when you and Mrs. Pembleton found DeLancey in the cemetery.''

The doctor seemed to sway, then regained his composure. He looked at DeLancey and offered a hesitant smile. ''I had hoped you would never find out about that.''

''But why?'' she asked. ''I thought the two of you cared about me.''

''We did. I still do,'' he insisted. ''I know what Esther and I did was wrong.''

''We all know that,'' Matt said. ''What we'd like to know is why.''

Reluctantly, the doctor led them to his office. ''Have a seat.''

Matt took DeLancey's hand as she sat on the edge of one of the wing chairs. She drew strength from his touch. It didn't seem possible that her first fifteen years were a blank and the last ten had been a lie.

''You have to understand,'' Dr. Howard began. ''Esther didn't find you in the best of circumstances.''

''Which still doesn't explain why you never filed a report.''

Dr. Howard seemed angered by Matt's pointed comment. ''If I may be given an opportunity to explain without interruption?''

''Please?'' DeLancey asked as she gave Matt's hand a squeeze.

Dr. Howard steepled his fingers beneath his chin. ''Esther and I fully intended to turn DeLancey over to the authorities as soon as she regained her memory.

I believed that if she was given an opportunity to rest, her memory would return in time. Complete amnesia is quite rare." He paused and let out a breath. "It was Esther's idea to tell everyone that you were the orphaned grandchild of an old friend."

"Why did she need an idea?" Matt asked.

"While we waited for DeLancey to regain her strength, we found out about a murder in Pontiac."

"I'm aware of that case," Matt said. "A man in his early twenties was stabbed to death."

The doctor nodded. "Exactly. At the time, the newspapers said they were looking for the man's young girlfriend. The only description was 'a small woman with dark hair.' The man had a history of arrests for rape. Though there was every possibility that anything DeLancey had done she had done in self-defense, Esther was insistent that she not face the authorities until her memory returned and she could adequately defend herself."

"Was there evidence of rape?" Matt asked.

"I didn't do that sort of exam," he said. "But the first few weeks, DeLancey barely spoke. She became agitated when touched. Classic symptoms to be expected in a case of sexual assault."

DeLancey felt faint. It was true. She was a killer.

"Are you okay?" Matt asked gently.

She shook her head.

"I'm sorry we lied to you," Dr. Howard said. "We thought we were protecting you."

"Why didn't you tell the sheriff about this when

Mrs. Pembleton and Gomez were murdered?'' Matt asked.

The doctor seemed genuinely shocked by the question. "Tell them what, Mr. Tanner? That DeLancey has spent years under the care of my oldest friend? During which she has never shown herself to be anything but a kind, loving girl?"

"You believed she killed someone ten years ago."

"No," he said as he got to his feet. "I believe she defended herself ten years ago, and nothing has happened in all that time to convince me otherwise. DeLancey," he said as he came around the desk, "it was my hope that you would never learn any of this. Now that you have, I hope you'll consider all your options before you make any rash decisions. Think about what you'll be throwing away. Think about who you are deep inside. No matter what happens, I'll be here for you."

Matt tugged her to her feet and led her from the office. "Are you taking me to the sheriff?" she asked.

"No."

His answer startled her out of her stupor. "But we know what I did."

"No," he said more insistently. "We know what Dr. Howard and Mrs. Pembleton believed you did. Until we go to Pontiac, we can't be sure."

"Why would he admit all that to me if it wasn't true? I remember I found some clippings about that murder in Mrs. Pembleton's things. I guess it makes sense."

Matt kissed her hand. "At best, it's a possibility. We'll go to Pontiac tomorrow and nose around."

"Then what?"

"Let's just follow the leads for now."

"THIS ISN'T a lead, it's unlawful entry," DeLancey whispered as they crept through Alan's dark law office.

Matt took the tiny flashlight out of his mouth and shushed her before replacing it and continuing to the front of the office.

"We're okay now. We can turn on the light."

"Won't we get caught?"

Matt groped the wall until he felt the switch and flipped it. "Calm down," he said. "If the sheriff does have this place under surveillance, they'll watch the back. These windows face the street."

"How do you know?"

"Because if I wanted to watch this place, I'd watch the back. There's no street parking, and I doubt they expect Alan to make the same long trek through the woods that we did. Can we start looking now?" Matt asked.

"I guess. What exactly am I supposed to look for?"

"Anything and everything that has to do with you, Mrs. Pembleton, Gomez, Dr. Howard or the estate."

"No problem," her heard her whisper as he went to the desk and opened the bottom drawer.

"Great." He groaned when he opened empty

drawer after empty drawer. "I guess the sheriff or the state police confiscated everything for evidence."

"Not everything," DeLancey said. "Look at these."

Matt went to the file cabinet and stood behind her to look inside the drawer. "There must be at least a hundred copies of this photograph of you in here," he said as he carefully thumbed through them with a gloved hand. "The cops took every scrap of paper out of here and left these. That doesn't make sense."

"What doesn't make sense," she said as she cowered against him, "is why Alan would steal the photograph from Mrs. Pembleton, make copies, then try to scare me witless with them."

"Maybe he thinks he can scare you off. Or maybe he had his flunky Stephen do it for him."

"But if what Dr. Howard said was true, then Alan didn't know about the cemetery or the other stuff. And forget Stephen. He only worked at the Columbia office. Besides, Alan fired him the day he read the second will. And can you see that brownnoser plotting anything this elaborate?"

"True. But Esther had ten years to confide in her cousin," Matt told her. "Though I still think if she had told him, he would have shared that instantly with the police."

"Then explain the pictures," DeLancey pleaded.

"I can't. Yet."

"So what do we do now?" she asked.

"We get a decent night's sleep and head to Pontiac in the morning."

"Is there a Plan B?"

Matt kissed her, since he didn't want to lie to her.

Chapter Fifteen

"Is anything familiar to you?" he asked as they passed the sign announcing their arrival in Pontiac, South Carolina.

"It isn't like that," she told him.

"What is it like?"

"Like going to get your eyes checked. I feel like one eye is covered."

"Do you ever have dreams that might be memories?"

"As if I'd know." She sighed. "Actually, I get a sense of a memory, not the real thing."

"Explain that to me."

"I remember feeling a sense of urgency. Sometimes I remember being afraid, especially when I'm around water."

"The stream behind the cemetery?" he asked.

"I don't know. I've walked every inch of the banks during the last ten years, but nothing seems to throw my brain into gear."

"Where does the stream come from?"

"God?"

"I meant its physical origin."

"I'd have to look at a map. I think it might come down from Lake Wateree. Why are we stopping here?" she asked, distracted. "I thought we would go to the police or the sheriff."

"Knowledge is power," he said as he parked in front of the public library. After feeding the meter, Matt took her inside and found two microfilm machines. "We know you arrived in Canfield on July twenty-ninth. So we'll peruse the *Pontiac Voice* starting on the twenty-ninth of that year."

"I can't wait."

Matt pressed his lips against her forehead, then handed her the cassettes. Luckily, Pontiac wasn't a large town, so the newspaper rarely printed more than two dozen pages on any given day. There were car ads, ads for farm equipment, land deals and the occasional mention of someone getting arrested for drunk and disorderly or a domestic dispute.

"Here it is," DeLancey whispered.

Scooting his chair next to hers, he began to read about the discovery of Wayne Terrell's body in the middle of some farmer's soybean field. Just as Dr. Howard had said, Wayne had an arrest record that practically started in the womb. Matt imagined few people had mourned his early demise.

"Go forward," he told DeLancey.

The machine whirred to the next day. There were reports of a young female suspect. Again, Dr. Howard's account was fairly accurate. Apparently Wayne had made no secret of his attraction to a local girl, Cora Mae Stump.

"Cora Mae Stump?" DeLancey said. "No wonder I blocked out my name."

"We don't know if it's your name," he insisted as he impatiently brushed her hand aside and took control of the machine.

He followed the story into early September. Cora Mae disappeared the night Wayne was killed. He had deep scratches on his face and back. Forensics led authorities to believe he had died during or shortly after a sexual encounter.

"This is making me ill," DeLancey whispered.

Hearing the pain in her voice, he held her hand and said, "I can do this alone. Why don't you go outside and get some air?"

"What if someone recognizes me as Cora Mae Murderer?"

"Look at this picture," he said, tapping the screen. "It's grainy, but I don't see any resemblance."

"Grainy?" DeLancey repeated. "That's an understatement. I can't tell if that's a picture of a person or a monkey."

"What do you want to do?"

"I'll take a walk, but only right around here."

"I'll hurry."

"Don't do it on my account," she said before slipping from the reference area.

It was bright and sunny and beautiful outside, the

complete opposite of the way DeLancey was feeling. She was sorry she had started all this. Somehow it was almost easier not knowing.

DeLancey kept her head down as she walked along the sidewalk. Cars went by in a fairly steady stream, though most seemed to be traveling through town. It was a lot like Canfield in many respects. Big old homes lined either side of the street. She could hear mowers and smell freshly cut grass. The shrill sound of children squealing with delight as they played was tempered by the soft breeze. Every now and then she would pass a house with a window open. She heard snippets of songs on radios or dialogue from a television set.

It all seemed so peaceful, so normal. Such a contrast to what was happening to her. Once Matt had conclusive proof that she had killed that man years ago, she'd probably have to go to jail. Her cooking skills would be put to use making gruel or hash in some horrible prison kitchen. She'd never see Rose or Shelby again. Never hold Shelby's children. Never have any children of her own.

DeLancey thought about walking away, putting one foot in front of the other until she was someplace else, someplace she wouldn't have to say goodbye to her life. Or goodbye to Matt.

She came to an open space and sat on the grass. Hugging her knees to her chest, she watched butterflies float from one clover blossom to the next.

She'd reached the point where she was too sad to

cry. She felt empty. She knew this moment was the leading edge of a storm that would wash away everything she had ever dared to hope for. Everything she had tried to make of herself.

She could imagine how the press would cover this. A chef convicted of carving up a rapist. She shuddered and watched one of the butterflies fly away.

When it landed on the ledge of a second-story window, DeLancey's mind flashed a vivid and terrible memory.

She was below the open window of a house with cedar-shake siding that had several coats of pale blue paint. The window was open, and the curtain was blowing half in and half out. The floral curtain from the yellow room. She was looking up when the blood splattered on the curtains.

That didn't make any sense, though. Wayne was found in a field. Maybe the curtains had been in the farmer's house? "So why am I looking up?" she whispered. "If I was the one doing the killing, why was the blood spattering when I was outside the house?"

Feeling equal measures of panic and exhilaration, DeLancey raced to the library. Matt was waiting for her on the steps.

"I know something," she called.

"Me, too."

DeLancey held the stitch in her side as she spoke before catching her breath. "I was outside when he was killed."

"Who?"

"Wayne, I guess. I was sitting down and feeling sorry for myself when I happened to look up. I saw part of the house and I saw the blood."

Matt took her to the car. "Slow down and tell me again."

"The house is old and wooden and had several coats of blue paint on the shakes. The yellow room is on the second floor."

"Do you have any idea where the house is?" he asked.

"Remote, I think. It must have been the farmhouse where Wayne was killed. But I don't think I did it," she said as she grasped fistfuls of his shirt. "I saw the blood hit the curtain when I was outside."

"That fits," Matt said.

"Fits what? What did you find?"

"I found out what happened to Cora Mae."

"What?"

"She died in a car accident three years ago."

DeLancey jumped into his arms. "Thank you! Thank God!"

Matt held her, then set her on the pavement. "We know you didn't kill Wayne. But we still don't know how you ended up in that cemetery with a knife."

DeLancey sobered. "True. So now what do we do?"

"Go to Canfield."

"Isn't that like starting over?" she asked.

"It's more like stepping back and taking a hard look at things."

"Like what?"

"Like, if Dr. Howard and Mrs. Pembleton suspected you killed Wayne, why didn't they know Wayne's murderer died?"

"Maybe it wasn't considered newsworthy in Canfield."

"Your hometown paper does leave a little to be desired in the useful-information department. But if the doctor and Mrs. Pembleton thought you were Cora Mae, wouldn't they have made some attempt to stay on top of the investigation?"

"Not if they thought I killed that man. You read the news articles. It sounds like Cora Mae performed a public service."

"DeLancey, my gut tells me you didn't end up in Canfield by accident. You might not have had a memory, but did you have a sense about Canfield? Something that might have drawn you there?"

She shook her head. "No, but I did get a strange feeling when I saw the blue house with the curtains."

"Fear?"

"Yes, but mostly I felt like I needed to go inside."

"Why would a fifteen-year-old want to go inside a house where she sees blood?"

"Her parents?" she asked.

"Possibly," Matt conceded. "Maybe a sibling. But I find it hard to believe that no one would have reported you missing if your parents had been attacked.''

''What if I attacked them?''

Matt put his hand on her knee. ''Then you would have been in the house, not outside watching.''

''I hope you're right.''

''So do I.''

When they arrived at the estate, there was a package from Dylan on the step and a note from Stephen Thomason taped to the door.

''He certainly is in a rush to come to your aid,'' Matt grumbled when he read the syrupy note asking her to come to his office as soon as possible to sign probate documents.

''He's probably just trying to do his job.''

Matt gave her a sidelong glance. ''Right, that's why he suggested you come alone and at the cocktail hour.''

She smiled. ''You sound jealous, Professor.''

''So shoot me.''

''You shouldn't really be jealous. It isn't like we can have anything permanent.'' Her expression grew somber. ''I've got too much baggage.''

''You don't have baggage, DeLancey, you just have a secret, a mystery. I'm going to solve it for you.''

She looked at him, puzzled. ''For *me?*''

''Of course, for you.''

''I'm beginning to think otherwise.''

"Meaning?" He stood with his legs apart, his arms crossed over his massive chest.

"I've always thought that my...incomplete past would make it impossible for me to have a meaningful, honest relationship."

"I'm sure it has."

She met his gaze and held it. "I've been honest with you."

"Not from the start."

She felt anger and frustration and...pain. "What about you? Thanks to Dylan, I've known since day one that you left the police force because you felt you should have prevented the death of your partner's wife, Jenny."

"I should have," he said quietly, stoically.

"We can debate your past all night, but right now, I'm more concerned about your motives."

"My motive is simple. I want to help you find the truth."

"My truth, or your penance?"

He sighed heavily. "You aren't making sense, DeLancey."

"I'm making perfect sense. You expect so much and yet you give so little."

"I've been there for you."

"Physically, definitely. Emotionally...sometimes."

He threw his hands up in an exasperated fashion. "What do you want from me?"

"I want to know that whatever we find out won't matter to you. I want to know that your faith and your feelings are about me now, not about someone who existed years ago.''

"I do have feelings for you, DeLancey.''

"Matt, I need more than feelings. I need you. All of you. And you can't give me that. Not now. Maybe not ever. And I won't settle for less.''

DeLancey turned and left him feeling stupefied. Facts and answers were his business. He'd never been comfortable with mysteries. Surely DeLancey understood that.

He needed a drink. He poured himself a brandy, drained the glass and poured another before he ripped into the package from Dylan.

In bold script, Dylan had scribbled, *This is harmless unless you're thinking of enlisting.*

He opened the envelope and found a second one inside. The address of the military school was typed in the upper corner. His name was typed, as well. Inside he found a yearbook from the school dating back ten years. Not exactly current. Someone in the school's recruiting office had made a mistake. Matt flipped through the book, looking at the photographs. He was near the end when he began to understand why he'd been sent the book. One picture was circled with red pen. He recognized the name, but not the significance.

"Hello again, Trevor Walsh, professor of history.''

Chapter Sixteen

"I swear to you, I've never been to the Carolina Military Academy, and I don't know Trevor Walsh," DeLancey insisted for the fifth time.

"Then why would someone send this to me?"

"Because you visited the school?"

"The envelope didn't have the school crest. I called this morning before you got up, and no one there ever heard of me."

She looked at him over the rim of her coffee mug. "Maybe *you* know Trevor Walsh. You're a professor. Don't you guys all get together and do professor stuff?"

"He's dead."

She took a sip of coffee. "How do you know that?"

"I saw a plaque in the school chapel."

"Yesterday I was Cora Mae Murderer, so today I must have killed some history professor from a school not forty miles from here? I'm too tired to confess to this one, Matt. I'm tired, period."

"What happened to your burning desire to know your past?"

She shrugged. "I know I didn't kill anyone."

"How do you know that? You were found with bloody clothes and a knife, DeLancey."

"I remember that part," she said as his accusing tone stabbed at her heart. "I've just decided that I don't care anymore. I want to go back to Charleston and forget all about this."

"What about the threatening phone calls and the pictures?"

"The ones we found in Alan's office?" She put her cup down hard. "Maybe I don't have all the pieces, Matt. But I don't care anymore. I've spent ten years atoning for a past I can't remember. I deliberately chose a career that would keep me in the shadows, always in the background. I've never allowed myself to have a close friend. I've never had a serious relationship."

"What am I?"

She shrugged. "That's something you'll have to decide for yourself."

"Cut me some slack, DeLancey! I love you! What more do you want?"

"A lot more, Matt. So let's just go home and forget about each other."

He looked as if steam would pour out of his ears at any moment. "It's that easy for you? But you've had practice, haven't you? If you don't like something, you just conveniently erase it."

"Direct hit, Professor. Now, when can we leave?"

"Later," he grumbled as he slammed out of the house. DeLancey decided it was just as well. She needed a good cry.

MATT REACHED the military academy in a worse mood than when he'd walked out on DeLancey. He should give her a call and apologize. And he would as soon as he figured out why someone had sent him that yearbook.

He approached a teenage guard and said, "I'm Professor Matthew Tanner from Glens Falls College in New York. Would it be possible for me to speak to your dean?"

"That would be Commander Jasper, sir."

"May I see him?"

The pencil-necked soldier went into his little booth and made a call. "The commander is reviewing a platoon right now, but his aide said you were welcome to wait in the office until the commander returns."

"Thank you."

"Follow the signs to the green lot. Park your vehicle there and proceed to the administration building."

"Thanks again."

"My pleasure, sir. Welcome to Carolina Military."

Matt wondered if he should yell *Semper Fi* out the window. Apparently this school turned fourteen-year-old boys into minimarines.

Matt parked where instructed and followed the signs to the administration building. He found the commander's office.

"I'm Matthew Tanner," he said as he introduced himself to a pimple-faced young man behind a huge desk.

"Welcome to Carolina Military, sir," the boy barked as he stood at rigid attention. "May I get you some refreshment while you wait?"

"Coffee?"

"Cream and sugar, sir?"

"Black," he answered, amazed that he was barking right back at the kid.

Matt choked down two cups of bitter chicory coffee before a giant man with about a sixteenth of an inch of gray hair entered the office. Matt and the boy stood at attention.

"Commander Jasper," he said, offering a chunky hand.

"Matthew Tanner." As he supplied his name, Matt had to look up to meet the officer's steady, assessing gaze. That didn't happen very often. "Thank you for seeing me without an appointment."

"More coffee?"

"No," Matt said quickly. "Thanks."

"Let's go into my office," the commander suggested.

The office suited the man. It was dark, neat and organized. Even the various animal trophies protruding from the walls looked respectful and tidy.

"I'd like to discuss a former faculty member with you."

"For what reason?"

Matt told him about his sabbatical and the topic of his doctoral research. "The name Trevor Walsh came up in my research."

"Why?"

Matt blinked. "I was under the impression that Dr. Walsh had died."

"Incorrect."

Matt crossed his legs and leaned closer. A few too many shells might have hurt the man's hearing. "There's a memorial plaque in the chapel."

"Correct."

He raked his hand through his hair. "Aren't memorial plaques usually a posthumous honorarium?"

"Not in this case." The commander checked his watch and stood up. "I'm afraid that's all the time I have, Professor Tanner."

"What about Dr. Walsh?"

"I don't believe I can assist you any further."

Matt left the commander's office reluctantly. If the commander didn't want to help him, he'd have to find someone who did. He had just the right person in mind.

"WELCOME BACK, sugar."

Matt smiled at the pink lady who guarded the newspaper archives in Camden. "Hello, again. I'm going to need your help again."

"My pleasure." She fairly purred.

"I need anything you have on Dr. Trevor Walsh."

She pursed her lips. "You sure, honey? I still get sick thinking about what than man did. And to think they put him in some loony bin instead of throwing him to a pack of mongrel dogs like he deserved."

"What exactly did he do?"

She shrank back. "He went nuts one day and killed his entire family. Kids and all."

"Do you remember when this happened?"

"Ten years ago last July. It was all over the papers. Some of us would go to his trial during our lunch break. I never did believe what that psychiatrist said. That man didn't have a psychotic break, he was just plain mean."

"I really need you to get those clippings for me," Matt said. "Is there a phone around here?"

"Pay phone up on the first floor. You sure you want everything?"

He nodded, then went to call DeLancey.

"IF HE ISN'T BACK in an hour, I'm going to rent a car and come home alone."

"Be patient," Shelby cautioned. "I'd much rather have you wait than have you on the roads all by yourself. Especially if someone tampered with your car once before."

"That is one of the main reasons I want to get out of here. I feel like the proverbial fish in the barrel."

"Is coming back here safe for you?"

DeLancey considered her answer. "I can't explain it, but I know in my heart that getting away from here is my best option."

"I thought you loved that place."

"I did," she admitted. "Let's just say I've outgrown my childhood home. Oops. There's someone at the door. I'll call you back before I leave so you won't worry."

"Please wait for Matt," Shelby urged.

"I will," she said, hung up the phone, then added, "for a while."

After a precautionary check out the window, DeLancey opened the door. "I'm glad you're here, Stephen."

"You are?" he asked.

"If you'll take me to Craig's gas station so I can rent a car, I'll sign whatever you want me to sign."

He seemed pleased, almost excited. "I, uh, I have the papers at my new office."

"Where is it?" she asked as she grabbed her bag and followed him down the stairs.

"Just outside town," he said. "I rented a house. I think you'll like it."

DeLancey didn't care if he had set himself up inside Miss Foster's greenhouse as long as he would give her a lift into town. While she wasn't Stephen's biggest fan, his company was better than her other option—hitchhiking. She wasn't stupid. She wouldn't put herself at the mercy of some stranger.

"Have you spoken to Alan?" she asked.

"He's still quite upset with me over the will."

DeLancey nodded as she fastened her seat belt. "I'm sorry if all this set your career back. But why did you rent a place outside Canfield if you're used to practicing in Columbia?"

"It's an easy commute," he said, his voice suddenly confident and strong. "Besides, I like the country. I've liked it ever since that first day when Mrs. Pembleton was dumb enough to let me inside her house."

DeLancey found herself staring at an almost unrecognizable face. His smile was so evil it was unreal. But his gun was very real. "Stephen, this doesn't make any sense. Why do you want to hurt me?"

"Sweet, sweet DeLancey," he said as he rubbed the cold steel revolver along her arm. "Or would you prefer me to call you Wendy?"

"Wendy?"

"That's your real name. Wendy Walsh. Personally, I think DeLancey suits you much better."

Wendy Walsh? The name wasn't the least bit familiar. "How do you know all this?"

"Our dear Esther was quite the pack rat, wasn't she?"

He split his attention between her and the road. Stephen kept his speed up, making it impossible for her to jump, even if she could manage to unhook the seat belt without his knowing.

"It's a straight shot to the house," he said.

"What house?"

He sighed. "I want it to be a surprise."

"This isn't smart, Stephen. Matt will—"

"Be in Camden chasing his tail," he finished. "When and if he puts it together, it will be too late."

"You can't kill me."

Stephen laughed. "That's the beauty of this whole situation. I can kill you and get away with it."

"You can't be sure of that," she warned, desperately hoping to plant a seed of doubt in his unbalanced mind.

"Yes, I can. Because technically, you're already dead."

"DELANCEY!" Matt's voice echoed through the plantation house unanswered. He checked all the bedrooms, then drove through the high grass searching for her.

Frustrated, he went to the house and called Dylan.

"He isn't here," Shelby said. "I'm glad you're with DeLancey. She said she was going to leave. I was afraid she'd find a car and—"

"She isn't here, Shelby. Tell me exactly what she said she was going to do." She did. Matt hung up, puzzled.

Knowing DeLancey wouldn't have been dumb enough to go off with a stranger, he thought about whom she would trust.

His first guess was Dr. Howard, but the doctor wasn't home when Matt called. Increasingly frantic, he headed into town, hoping to find DeLancey at the luncheonette.

"Miss Foster!" he called, stopping his car in the middle of the street next to where she was walking. "Have you seen DeLancey?"

"Not for a while. Why?"

"I really can't explain right now. Where was she when you saw her? Was she with Dr. Howard?"

"No. He's at the hospital. DeLancey and that young attorney left town about an hour ago."

"Which way?"

"North, toward the hospital."

He wasn't sure if he thanked the woman and he didn't much care. He knew he had to get to DeLancey before Dr. Howard killed her.

"CAN I HELP YOU?" The nurse at the front desk of the hospital eyed him with professional concern. No surprise, thought Matt. His blood pressure was probably close to critical.

"Where is Dr. Howard?"

"Do you have an emergency, sir?" the nurse asked.

"I will if I don't find Dr. Howard in the next few seconds," Matt threatened, leaning his torso over the counter. "Page him. Now."

The nurse froze.

Matt gave up on waiting and began running down the corridor, calling for Dr. Howard. He soon arrived, along with two security guards.

"Mr. Tanner?"

Though he would have gladly decked the guy, he'd wait until he had DeLancey first. "Did the prosecutor in Camden know Trevor Walsh was your late wife's son from her first marriage when you testified on his behalf at his sanity hearing? The one I've been reading about all afternoon? I didn't see that mentioned in the transcripts."

Howard blanched and took Matt into a corner cubicle away from the eyes and ears of the crowd that was gathering. "No. Why are you asking about this?"

"I want to know what you've done with De-Lancey—or Wendy—or whatever you call her."

"I haven't seen her. Wendy?"

"Yes, Wendy—not Cora Mae, but you knew that all along, didn't you?"

The doctor blanched. "Yes, I just prayed she would never learn the truth. I did it for her own protection."

"Right," Matt said, seething.

"I did! I never wanted her to know that she had witnessed the murder of her entire family!"

"Not her *entire* family."

"I thought it was best if those memories stayed buried. It was safer for her. I never dreamed Esther would confide in Alan and he would go after her."

"Nice try, but I've already called the sheriff, and Alan Faircloth is hiding inside his house in Columbia. You're the only person alive who has known all along who DeLancey is. I don't know why you killed the old lady or Gomez. I don't understand why you tried to blow DeLancey to pieces with a car bomb, but if so much as one hair on her head is—"

"Dear Lord," Howard said as he fell against the wall. "It isn't me. I've never said a word. That was the deal I made with Esther. In exchange for taking DeLancey in after the incident—"

"Seeing her father kill her mother and her two brothers is an incident?"

"Esther's only condition was that it would be her decision when and if DeLancey was ever told the truth."

"The letter," Matt thought aloud. "She must have written it all down for DeLancey, only it never got delivered." Matt's mind raced. Who else could have had access to that letter? There was only one person. "Stephen Thomason. Where would he take her?"

"He once asked me about some property of mine up by the lake," Howard said. "I told him I didn't go up there any longer."

"Why?"

"Because of Trevor. The house was—"

"The address! Now!"

"I WON'T SIGN THEM." DeLancey glared at Stephen. "You'll kill me, but you won't get access to Mrs. Pembleton's estate."

"I've already transferred a lot of the cash. Once I probate the will, I'll have total control as the executor."

"It won't do you any good. Someone will figure out what you've done."

He smiled at her. "Matt? Dr. Howard? I don't think so. Matthew Tanner doesn't know the relationship between the doctor and your father. Incidentally, does this place bring back not-so-fine memories?"

She glanced around the room where Stephen had held her captive for almost an hour. The wallpaper was faded and peeling. The air was thick, musty and fuzzy with cobwebs. "Sorry, Stephen, but if part of your plan was for this house to spook me into submission, you failed."

He seemed only mildly disappointed. "No matter. I just thought it would be…poetic for you to die in the same house you were supposed to have died in years ago."

"I'll die without signing those papers."

He stepped forward, obviously running out of patience. "I've taken care of everything. The old lady and Gomez are dead. Alan will go to jail based on evidence I've planted. In a few weeks, Dr. Howard will take a terrible fall in his house. And I'll have full control of dear Esther's fortune. She really wanted you to have everything, but she couldn't find a way to tell you without exposing her dirty little deal with Howard. By the way, DeLancey Jones was more to Esther than just a name. It was the name she had given to her only child, a stillborn daughter conceived out of wedlock. The Tillmans insisted the gravestone not include the child's parentage. She didn't want you to know the truth about your past because the old bird really did love you. She wanted to protect you to the very end. However, once I explained that she could change her will or I would tell you everything, she agreed. I had a feeling she might renege on the deal, so I stepped up the poison. It was simple. I just slipped a little rat poison I'd lifted from Doctor Howard's greenhouse into her sugar bowl every time I visited. It was another moment of brilliance on my part. If that bozo sheriff in Canfield found the poison, he could easily trace it to Dr. Howard. Or should I say Granddaddy?'' He paused long enough to give a theatrical sigh and run the gun along his chin as if scratching an itch. "Really, it was too easy. I'd have preferred more of a challenge. But I'll make the best of it.''

DeLancey stared at his bland, preppie face, now set with a kind of mad fury. It was true. He was going to kill her. She was going to die.

"Make the best of this!" Matt yelled as he flew through the window and knocked Stephen to the ground. "Get the gun!" he yelled.

DeLancey raced in the direction the gun had gone when Matt knocked Stephen to the ground. She found it and spun to see Stephen straddling Matt, holding a thick board, ready to swing.

Aiming carefully, DeLancey closed her eyes and squeezed the trigger.

Epilogue

"Hi," DeLancey said, standing at the door of Matt's hospital room. "Can I come in?"

He smiled. "So long as you aren't armed." He winced when he laughed. "I wouldn't want you to shoot me again."

DeLancey blushed. "I didn't mean to shoot you. I was aiming for Stephen."

"I'm not complaining. You scared him so badly he ran out of that house and into the waiting arms of the sheriff." Matt reached out to her, urging her closer. "How are you doing?"

She shrugged. "I'm not sure yet. I'm still trying to understand everything."

"It's a lot to understand," he agreed as he took her hand and brought it to his lips. "Need some help getting through it?"

"I'm not sure how I'm going to deal with it. Apparently Dr. Howard has kept Trevor Walsh sedated for ten years. I have a hard time thinking of him as my father."

"Nothing has come back?"

She shook her head. "Dr. Howard told me Trevor Walsh's mental health had been declining for years. Apparently he snapped one night when I was fifteen. I was at a friend's house."

"Thank God for that," Matt said softly.

"Apparently, I went in the house, struggled with him, took the knife and ran."

"Why didn't the cops look for you?"

She shrugged. "I was cut during the struggle. They decided from finding my blood at the scene that Trevor Walsh had killed me first and hidden my body so the rest of the family wouldn't get suspicious."

"I read the transcripts of the sanity hearing. Dr. Howard testified that Walsh had admitted killing you during one of their sessions."

"I suppose that was his way of trying to protect me. At least that's what he said."

"Have you seen your father?"

She shook her head. "In a perverse way, I've decided Trevor Walsh succeeded in killing Wendy Walsh ten years ago."

"I agree."

"I didn't come here to tell you the sordid facts. I really wanted to apologize for shooting you and for disrupting your life."

He pulled her closer and looked deeply into her eyes. "I've decided to make some changes in my life. My outlook."

She hated the fact that she still held on to that last

thread of hope, that Matt had fallen in love with her, the real her. She didn't let her disappointment show. Instead, she feigned cheerfulness and asked, "Turning over a new leaf after your near-death experience at my hands?"

"Someone once told me that I didn't know how to love unconditionally."

"It's okay," she said, tugging at her hand to no avail. "We don't have to do this, Matt. I understand."

"I don't think you do. I guess my experience before I left the force changed me. I thought I knew my partner inside and out. It really shook me to discover that he wasn't the man I thought he was."

"That's understandable. I guess you can never really know a person."

"But it's worth the gamble, DeLancey. I lost sight of that for a little while. When I saw Thomason taunting you with that gun, I knew that whatever happened, I wanted you in my life. You've had my love since the first day I saw you at the Rose Tattoo. I know I didn't give you my unconditional trust, but that's only because I was afraid of making a mistake. I was afraid of giving everything without some guarantee for the future. Focusing on the past kept me from planning a future. I'm just sorry it took seeing you in danger to realize that."

"You're rambling."

"I'm trying to tell you that I know you have some baggage, and I don't care. I have some of my own."

"I have a life in Charleston. You're a New Yorker."

Matt shrugged. "I can teach anywhere. Besides, according to a very intelligent, very strong woman, I'm going to publish my research, go out on a book tour and be the darling of all the talk shows."

"Matt?"

"Yes?"

"Can you put the book tour off until after you marry me?"

He smiled, pulled her down and kissed her with tenderness. DeLancey knew then she was connected. Forever.

*And there's more
ROSE TATTOO!*

Turn the page for a hint of what's in store
for you in the next Rose Tattoo book
by Kelsey Roberts, coming to you in
January 1999.

WANTED: COWBOY

*Only from Kelsey Roberts and
Harlequin Intrigue!*

Prologue

"Is everything all set?"

"To the last detail."

"Are you sure?"

"Quit worrying. I'm on top of things."

"I don't know why you can't do this yourself. You aren't exactly the most ethical person I've ever encountered."

"I don't remember you complaining when you took the money."

"Money was one thing. This is different."

"This will make us rich."

"If we don't get caught."

"We won't. But we will be rich."

They shared a laugh in the darkness of the secluded park.

"What about Landry? Will he be a problem?"

"No."

"Who else will be there?"

"All twenty members of the board. How are you going to do it?"

"The less you know the better. Suffice to say it wouldn't be prudent for me to do this alone. The few people who know are—"

"What! How many people are involved? More people means more opportunity for someone to point the finger at us."

"Quiet! There's no way anyone will ever connect us. It isn't like I can pull the trigger myself. I had no choice but to hire a professional."

"We're going to get caught."

"Not if you keep your cool and do exactly what I said. Everything else has been arranged."

"When do I get my money?"

"In a hurry?" A humorless laugh accompanied the question.

"I wouldn't be doing this otherwise. I need the cash as soon as possible."

"And you'll get it."

"When?"

"When the target is…eliminated."

Catch more great

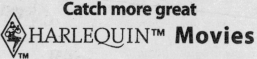 **HARLEQUIN™ Movies**

featured on

Premiering August 8th
The Waiting Game
Based on the novel by *New York Times*
bestselling author Jayne Ann Krentz

Don't miss next month's movie!
Premiering September 12th
A Change of Place
Starring Rick Springfield and
Stephanie Beacham. Based on the novel
by bestselling author Tracy Sinclair

If you are not currently a subscriber to
The Movie Channel, simply call your
local cable or satellite provider for more
details. Call today, and don't miss out
on the romance!

 **HARLEQUIN®**
Makes any time special ™

100% pure movies.
100% pure fun.

To my darling grandchildren,
I leave you my love and more. Within thirty-three
days of your thirty-third birthday, you will have in
your grasp a legacy of which your dreams are made.
Dreams are not always tangible things, but more
often born in the heart. Act selflessly in another's
behalf and my legacy shall be yours.

Your loving grandmother,
Moira McKenna

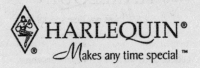

Share in the legacy of a lifetime!

Donovan Wilde lives an isolated, lone-wolf life. But after a murder brings publicity to his wildlife retreat, Donovan is about to discover he is the long-lost fourth McKenna grandchild. But will he return to the Donovan family and claim his legacy?

Don't miss Patricia Rosemoor's special return to the McKenna Family you love:

NEVER CRY WOLF

September 1998

Available at your favorite retail outlet.

HARLEQUIN®
Makes any time special ™

Award-winning author

Gayle Wilson

writes timeless historical novels and
cutting-edge contemporary stories.

Watch for her latest releases:

HONOR'S BRIDE—September 1998
(Harlequin Historical, ISBN 29032-2)

*A Regency tale of a viscount who falls for the courageous wife
of a treacherous fellow officer.*

and

NEVER LET HER GO—October 1998
(Harlequin Intrigue, ISBN 22490-7)

*A thriller about a blinded FBI agent and the woman assigned
to protect him who secretly carries his child.*

Available at your favorite retail outlet.

MEN at WORK

All work and no play?
Not these men!

July 1998
MACKENZIE'S LADY by Dallas Schulze

Undercover agent Mackenzie Donahue's
lazy smile and deep blue eyes were his best
weapons. But after rescuing—and kissing!—
damsel in distress Holly Reynolds, how could
he betray her by spying on her brother?

August 1998
MISS LIZ'S PASSION by Sherryl Woods

Todd Lewis could put up a building with ease,
but quailed at the sight of a classroom! Still,
Liz Gentry, his son's teacher, was no battle-ax,
and soon Todd started planning some
extracurricular activities of his own....

September 1998
A CLASSIC ENCOUNTER
by Emilie Richards

Doctor Chris Matthews was intelligent, sexy
and *very* good with his hands—which made
him all the more dangerous to single mom
Lizette St. Hilaire. So how long could she
resist Chris's special brand of TLC?

Available at your favorite retail outlet!

MEN AT WORK™

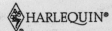 HARLEQUIN®   Silhouette®

Look us up on-line at: http://www.romance.net

PMAW2

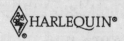

Not The Same Old Story!

Exciting, glamorous romance stories that take readers around the world.

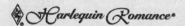

Sparkling, fresh and tender love stories that bring you pure romance.

Bold and adventurous— Temptation is strong women, bad boys, great sex!

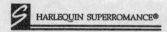

Provocative and realistic stories that celebrate life and love.

Contemporary fairy tales—where anything is possible and where dreams come true.

Heart-stopping, suspenseful adventures that combine the best of romance and mystery.

Humorous and romantic stories that capture the lighter side of love.

Keep up with KELSEY ROBERTS and

Be sure you've read all the books in this bestselling continuity series.

Rose Tattoo™

#22326	UNSPOKEN CONFESSIONS	$3.50 U.S.☐	$3.99 CAN.☐
#22330	UNLAWFULLY WEDDED	$3.50 U.S.☐	$3.99 CAN.☐
#22334	UNDYING LAUGHTER	$3.50 U.S.☐	$3.99 CAN.☐
#22349	HANDSOME AS SIN	$3.50 U.S.☐	$3.99 CAN.☐
#22395	THE TALL, DARK ALIBI	$3.75 U.S.☐	$4.25 CAN.☐
#22412	THE SILENT GROOM	$3.75 U.S.☐	$4.25 CAN.☐
#22429	THE WRONG MAN	$3.75 U.S.☐	$4.25 CAN.☐
#22455	HER MOTHER'S ARMS	$3.99 U.S.☐	$4.50 CAN.☐

(quantities may be limited on some titles)

TOTAL AMOUNT	$
POSTAGE & HANDLING	$
($1.00 for one book, 50¢ for each additional)	
APPLICABLE TAXES*	$ _____
TOTAL PAYABLE	$ _____
(check or money order—please do not send cash)	

To order, complete this form and send it, along with a check or money order for the total above, payable to Harlequin Books, to: **In the U.S.:** 3010 Walden Avenue, P.O. Box 9047, Buffalo, NY 14269-9047; **In Canada:** P.O. Box 613, Fort Erie, Ontario, L2A 5X3.

Name: _____

Address: _____ City: _____

State/Prov.: _____ Zip/Postal Code: _____

Account #: _____ 075 CSAS

*New York residents remit applicable sales taxes.
Canadian residents remit applicable GST and provincial taxes.

HARLEQUIN®
Makes any time special ™

HARLEQUIN®

I N T R I G U E®

COMING NEXT MONTH

#481 MARRIED IN HASTE by Dani Sinclair
A handsome stranger swept McKella Patterson out of the way of a speeding truck—then said her new husband was an impostor and her life was in danger. Truth gleamed from his eyes, and McKella's heart raced at his touch—but when the danger passed, would he disappear from her life as quickly as he'd entered it?

#482 FIRST-CLASS FATHER by Charlotte Douglas
Return to Sender
Unresolved conflict had made Heather Taylor leave Dylan Wade, the drop-dead-gorgeous cop she would always love. Desperation forced her to return. Despite their past, Dylan *had* to save her kidnapped baby—though he could *never* tell him the child was his own.

#483 NEVER CRY WOLF by Patricia Rosemoor
The McKenna Legacy
Donovan Wilde was a lone wolf who had no use for his McKenna blood, or the legacy that accompanied it. But when Laurel Newkirk showed up claiming to have been engaged to him—or someone pretending to be him—he knew he couldn't escape Grandmother Moira McKenna's legacy....

#484 ONLY A MEMORY AWAY by Madeline St. Claire
Were Judd Maxwell's recurring nightmares actually memories of a crime of passion? Beautiful social worker Karen Thomas wanted to help him unlock the memories—and his heart. But once unleashed, what would his memory reveal?

AVAILABLE THIS MONTH:

#477 UNFORGETTABLE NIGHT
Kelsey Roberts

#478 PRIORITY MALE
Susan Kearney

#479 THE RUNAWAY BRIDE
Adrianne Lee

#480 A ONE-WOMAN MAN
M.L. Gamble

Look us up on-line at: http://www.romance.net